The Redacted Sherlock Holmes Volume IX

By

Orlando Pearson

Paperback ISBN 978-1-80424-632-0
ePub ISBN 978-1-80424-633-7
PDF ISBN 978-1-80424-634-4

Published by MX Publishing
335 Princess Park Manor, Royal Drive,
London, N11 3GX
www.mxpublishing.co.uk

Cover design Awan

Contents

Alma

The first years of the new century brought forth a plethora of new cases for my friend, Mr Sherlock Holmes. In the works published in my lifetime I have always recounted his cases as separate events, but my reader will be unsurprised to learn that they often overlapped. In this period, he often had had three or even four cases under investigation at the same time. The workload this created took its inevitable toll on his normally iron constitution, and his behaviour became increasingly irregular. He ignored my pleas to take a rest, and it was only when Dr Moore Agar, of Harley Street, whose dramatic introduction to Holmes I may some day recount, gave positive injunctions that Holmes lay aside all cases if he wished to avert an absolute breakdown, that he agreed to take the waters.

My readers may at this point wonder what I now have to tell although a similar medical injunction had already given rise to the matter I have chronicled as *The Devil's Foot* of 1897. The matter that follows occurred in September 1903, but I have taken steps to ensure that the notes I set down here should not be read until long after both I, and the lady referred to in the title above, have departed this life. On this work's completion I will add it to those already in the tin despatch-case deposited in the strong room of my bankers, Cox & Co., with the clear injunction that it is not opened until her death and her youth means it is likely to succeed mine by several years.

Readers may think it remarkable that the relationship between Holmes and me should never have been impacted by strains over money or women in the two or more decades that we shared quarters in Baker Street, such being oft the fate of men who arrange their lives in the way that Holmes and I did.

For money Holmes had his detective practice which brought its rewards while I was able to live quite comfortably from the proceeds of the sale of my practice in Paddington which Holmes had brokered. Where money fell short, as these works which have been withheld from publication until after my death have already revealed, both Holmes and I had skills which we could use for our financial benefit.

Some may wonder how a woman or women might ever be a factor in our relationship as I married twice while Holmes described himself in *The Valley of Fear* as "not the marrying kind." But being "not the marrying kind" is not the same thing as being without feeling for women as shown by his bestowal of the soubriquet, "*The* Woman" on Irene Adler. In the case I describe now, things went considerably further than they did with Frau Adler, and this work describes an instance where either Holmes's feelings for a woman or more openness of my part might have caused a permanent rift in our friendship. There will also be readers who feel that Holmes and I might and should have behaved differently from what is disclosed here. There are thus several different reasons why this work is being recorded for posterity but held back until the moment for its publication is right.

Holmes had eventually decided on Baden bei Wien, sixteen miles to the south of Vienna, capital of the Austro-Hungarian empire, as the place to take the waters. I confess to being something of a sceptic on the health benefits of the consumption of water containing naturally occurring but foul-tasting salts, but Baden is the German-speaking part of Austria's biggest resort, and consequently boasts both a theatre and a casino and so, even if I felt no benefit from the waters, I was never going to succumb to boredom.

Whenever I could, I avoided the consumption of water and associated treatments and instead walked the countryside around Baden. On the first full day I climbed to the highest point of the Spa Park, the Kalvarienberg, or Calvary Mountain, from where I enjoyed splendid views. I confess I felt a slight frisson of *Schadenfreude* or joy at the travails of another as I thought of Holmes and the Calvary of his own he was going through as he underwent the prescribed medicinal treatments somewhere below me.

On the evening of the second day, we made the short journey into central Vienna, where Holmes had got us front-row seats at the city's main concert-hall, the Musikverein. We heard a performance of Beethoven's *Choral Symphony* with the director of the Court Opera, Gustav Mahler, guest-conducting the Vienna Philharmonic and its Choir. These combined forces sounded in the finale as though they were storming the gates of heaven as they performed Schiller's *An die Freude* or *Ode to Joy*. Indeed, such was their vigour, it rendered a full understanding of the text unnecessary.

On the third day of our sojourn, I came down to breakfast and found that Holmes was yet to appear. Accordingly, I delayed placing my order and practised my German on the local newspapers while I waited for him. Time passed rapidly, and it was only after a quarter of an hour that I asked the waiter if he had seen my friend.

"I saw your companion," said Putschandl in the sing-song way the Viennese pronounce English, "on his way into breakfast a few minutes before you. But, as he was coming in here, he was approached by a dark-haired man with glasses.. I saw them go down the front stairs of the hotel together and get into a….Droschke.." he paused and wrinkled his brow while he considered what might be the right word in English... "a cab. I expect they went to the station."

My heart sank.

Could Holmes have been sufficiently unguarded to take on a new case when a physician of much greater repute than I had instructed him to rest? And if not, what else might he be up to? My waiter was unable to provide any more information, and I decided to order breakfast as I had no means of knowing where Holmes had gone, let alone when he would be back.

I was addressing myself to some excellent fare when a woman came to me and explained that due to an error in table allocations, there was no table free for her. She asked if she could join me at mine as I had a place free.

My German was sufficient to the task of understanding what she was saying but it soon became apparent that the

English of this bright, quick woman in her mid-twenties, her face freckled like a plover's egg, and the manner of one who had her own way to make in the world, was better than my German. I looked around and pointed out that two other tables were unoccupied.

"I fear that they are reserved for other guests for all that they are empty now," said she in the same sing-songy tone which the waiter had adopted, though this time with a honeyed tone that was all its own. As I watched, a waiter walked over to one of tables I had pointed out, and put a Reserved sign on it.

"Very well, madame" said I, somewhat at a loss at the turn of events and not wishing to make any sort of a scene, "then you may sit at my table as the anticipated occupant of the second seat will probably not be joining me."

She sat down and the waiter brought her a breakfast menu.

I studied her as well and as discreetly as I could from behind my newspaper. She seemed to be reading from a note and a variety of expressions – hurt and anger, I hazarded – crossed her fair countenance. But then she surprised me with a glance in my direction and a look of serenity came over her face. I had, I suddenly realised, been slow to note that she was something of a beauty and, as she bore no ring on her left hand so, I could only assume, she was unmarried. As my reader will be aware, at this time I had been widowed for about ten years, and hence there was no impropriety if I chose to engage in discussions with an apparently unattached woman in a public place although no conversational gambit would come to my mind.

"And what brings you here?" she asked, interrupting my reflections.

"I am here with a friend who has been seriously over-taxing himself," I said cautiously. "I fear I do not know where he is at present, and I have no means of finding out."

"Ah!" said she with a hint of a sigh, "personal stress and anxieties are a bane of the modern age. I too am here as I fear life has become all too much for me."

She sighed again, and though the ambience was not particularly warm, she fanned herself with a languorous air. As the fan flickered to and fro, I observed she had a diamond ring on the fourth finger of her right-hand. Did married women in Austria wear their wedding rings on their left or right hand, I wondered. I could not be sure and so stimulating did our conversation rapidly become that I put the question to one side along with my newspaper which I put down with the words, "Nothing much to read in here today, I fear."

"Indeed," replied she, shaking her dark tresses, "it feels very much as if the world can get along perfectly well without us, when we are in isolation here south of Vienna. This is quite a different world. And all the better for it."

At this moment the waiter came back, and my fair interlocutor placed her order.

I was slightly startled to see when it arrived that her breakfast included a glass of sparkling wine, and she raised it in toast to me.

"Ein Glas Sekt," she said with a sparkle in her eye that outdid even the wine's effervescence, "schmeckt."

She put the glass to her beautiful lips and the wine seemed to chase away any final cares she might have had. So, I concluded, a glass of sparkling wine in German was "Ein Glas Sekt," and I was to learn that "schmeckt" meant "tastes good." Not many more minutes passed before I had ordered a glass of Sekt of my own and I could think of nothing I wanted to do more than raise it in toast to my fair table companion. The unexpected absence of Holmes suddenly seemed but a fleeting annoyance – he was absent for weeks on end often enough when we were in Baker Street – and now I focused my attention on this nameless lady sitting at my table.

Conversation flowed.

"I have heard the theory," she opined after a few minutes as she delicately raised the glass to her lips once more, "that bubbles from sparkling wine taste even better when one is at altitude."

This thesis was news to me.

I confined myself to commenting, perhaps a little drily, "I fear, dear lady, that it will be difficult to test that hypothesis here in Baden. I have climbed the Kalverienberg, the highest point for fifty miles around. It is only just over one thousand feet, and we are considerably lower than that here in our hotel. The nearest proper mountains are in Styria, many, many miles away."

"I have been told," my interlocuter replied steadily, a sudden note of sweetness coming into her voice, and her beautiful chestnut eyes, as they looked deep into mine, penetrating the depths of my soul, "that even elevation by a mere couple of floors can make all the difference."

I paused to consider this remark.

I had not yet responded when she added in a tone of aching loveliness, "My quarters are on the second floor if you would like to join me in putting what I have said to the test."

As my reader will have realised, seduction had not been part of my plans at the start of the morning but – maybe the frisson from the rapidly ascending bubbles of my wine helped – I was more than happy to be swept off my feet by my new acquaintance whose name I still had not thought to ask for just as she had not asked for mine. If these words are ever read, my more adult readers may form their own views on what happened next. It is in any case my hope that they make sure this work is kept out of the hands of anyone not yet sufficiently versed in the ways of the world just as the case of *The Giant Rat of Sumatra* has been held back until the world is ready.

The next thing that I can recall was being woken from the deepest and sweetest slumber by a cleaner banging on the door. When I looked round, it was to see the room empty not only of my fair companion but also of any of the impedimenta she might have had. I dressed as quickly as I could and bolted through the door, past the cleaner, and down the corridor to make my way to the sanctuary of my own room on the floor below.

Once I had gained the solitude of my quarters, the events of the morning made me feel as happy as I had ever been.

Indeed, as I recalled what had happened but a short time previously, a smile of the broadest satisfaction came across my face. In Holmes's absence I felt no need to do anything other than please myself for the rest of the day, and I took another walk up the Kalvarienberg, and, if the truth be told, put what I rather feared would be my fleeting acquaintance's theory about the consumption of sparkling wine at altitude to the test at the mountain's summit. For the curious, I can confirm that my Sekt did taste particularly sweet although whether that was because of the events of the morning or my elevated location I could not say.

It was about nine o'clock in the evening that I returned to the hotel. The events of the day had made me feel so good I had determined to retire to bed with no more than some more Sekt inside me – two glasses, I thought, rather than one – but in the hotel lobby was Sherlock Holmes evidently fresh returned from wherever he had been. My regular readers will know my friend as a man who has made his living out of his self-confidence, and it was something of a shock to see him now looking completely unsure of himself. In the exchange the follows below his mien lurched from a look of supreme satisfaction to one of unprecedented self-doubt.

"Well," said he, not meeting my eye, "I suppose that as you are my biographer I had better give you my version of the events of the day."

I was not sure how to respond to this and retained a studied silence.

"As I was going into breakfast this morning," said Holmes, "a dark-haired man with glasses darted up to me. I would put him in his mid-forties. His anxiety to speak to me was obvious."

"Pray continue," I said to Holmes, and I set out below what he had to recount with some interjections from me.

> "Mr Holmes," said the man, "I am the conductor Gustav Mahler. I thought when I looked out from the conductor's podium into the audience in the Musikverein last night that it was you I saw applauding in the front row and it as well that I have the chance to speak to you out of the presence of your friend, Dr Watson, as I have a matter to present to you which requires the utmost discretion."

"Pray continue," I said.

> "I am a subscriber to *The Strand* magazine which is sent to me from London every issue and I always turn first to the pages about you when I receive it. The pictures in the magazine give, if I may say so, a very accurate reflection of what you look like. And now I find you where you are staying."

"The reason why I had chosen Baden bei Wien as the place for our sojourn, good Watson," said my friend addressing me, "was that it offered the healing springs that my doctors had recommended, enough to keep me entertained while I was avoiding casework, and a language I spoke well enough to quote from its poetry and aphorisms at length. Being recognised was not a hazard I had reckoned with. I was still weighing up my response when my interlocuter continued."

> "My wife is taking the waters here while I stay in Vienna for my conducting," said Mahler, "and I had agreed to come down from Vienna this morning and join her for breakfast. It is a happy coincidence indeed that I should find she is staying at the same hotel as you are."

> I remain unsure even now what I was going to say but Herr Mahler continued almost without a break.

> "I have a case of the most pressing personal concern, and I would like you to come back with me to Vienna."

"But Holmes," exclaimed I, "you had specific instructions to undertake no case work for your health."

"I fear, good Watson," replied Holmes looking slightly uneasy, "that the call of the chase was too strong. In less than a few minutes, Herr Mahler and I were in a cab, a few minutes more saw us at Baden's station where Mahler went briefly into the telegraph office. A few minutes after that and we were in the first-class compartment of the train back to Vienna with Mahler speaking to me *sotto voce*."

Holmes continued.

> "I first met my wife in December 1901," said Mahler. "I was already forty and she a mere twenty-two. We married within three months of

our first meeting. She is intelligent, educated, beautiful, and dashing."

Mahler paused as though he were expecting a comment from me, but I confined myself to saying, "Pray continue."

"The first child, Maria, arrived in November 1902."

"So, your wife may have been with child when you married and I note you refer to Maria, born in November 1902, as 'the' child leaving open the possibility that it was a child of which you were not the father."

"That is so," said Mahler. "I confess things seemed to happen so quickly with Alma that I hardly knew what to make of them."

"What is the state of your marriage now."

"My wife is attentive to my every need. Before she met me, she composed music, she sang, she wrote about music, and hers was the name every host of every major social gathering in Vienna wanted to have on their guest list."

"I fear that you have not answered my question."

"Mr Holmes, I am a genius," said the maestro with a sudden earnestness that I found disconcerting. "Just as you are. Indeed, as you are to detective work, so am I to music. I require a wife whose every engagement is dedicated to me. Accordingly on our marriage I forbade her to compose, to sing, or to write. I insisted that she run our household so that I have nothing to do except work and that she come to the Opera House every evening to pick me up. And she does. Were you to marry, Mr Holmes," – I raised my eyebrows at this unlikely prospect – "I am sure you would arrange things in much the same way with your wife who has fulfilled my every demand."

"It is you who have engaged me in this matter, Maestro," I replied. "It is not the other way round. You have now made the state of your marriage clear. My situation is of no relevance here. What is it you want me to do?"

"My wife is a copious diarist. I cannot get the idea out of my head that the child with which she presented me half a year ago is not in fact my own. I want you to go through her diaries while she is in Baden bei Wien taking the waters and identify where she was and whom she was seeing at the time nine months before the arrival of Maria."

"Why can you not do that yourself if she is in Baden and you are in Vienna?"

"My wife keeps her diaries under lock and key in her desk. I need you to break the locks, read the diaries, draw your conclusions, and put the diaries back as they were so that my wife is unaware of what has happened. I have read your works with great ardour, and I know that you are the only man in the world who can provide the technical skills to do this, has the plausibility to make any charges that might arise stick, and the discretion to make sure that whatever I decide to do does not become public knowledge. It is a wonder indeed that I should come to Baden to the precise hotel where you are staying."

"What are your plans for the day?"

"I will be at rehearsals during the day and performing this evening. My wife will come to the Opera House to pick me up after I have given tonight's performance of Beethoven's opera *Fidelio* – ach, the irony of performing an opera about faithfulness in my present situation."

"But," I exclaimed, "you would have had no means to break a safe and return its contents apparently untouched."

For answer Holmes gave a slightly wan smile and drew from an inside pocket a small black leather case. He opened it to reveal a veritable mini-arsenal of safe breaking equipment.

"I am never without this. Or my pistol."

"What happened next?" I asked, and Holmes continued.

By now the train had drawn into Vienna's south station.

"How will your wife react to your failure to join her at breakfast this morning?" I asked.

"When I was in the telegraph office," replied Mahler, "I left a message at the hotel for her that I had been detained by work in Vienna. She is used to my work taking precedence over all other matters."

"Will I be undisturbed at your house while I search? A man of your standing will have a domestic staff at home."

"In the telegraph office, I also thought to leave a message to my staff saying I needed quiet at home and giving them the day off. They are used to my work taking precedence over all other matters."

"You seem to have thought it all out perfectly."

"It is much like conducting an opera, Mr Holmes. Everything must be in the right place at the right time," said Mahler.

Soon a cab had brought us to the Mahlers' elegant quarters in the Auenbruggergasse at the north end of Schloss Belvedere Park close to the centre of Vienna.

"There is her desk," said Mahler, pointing to a large mahogany escritoire in a study. "It is locked, its legs are screwed to the floor, and its back to the wall. It has a built-in safe into which she secrets her diary every night after she has made her entries. I do not know how many volumes are in there for she seems to get a new notebook every few months, but it is the entries from 1901 that I would wish you to focus on."

The conductor glanced at his watch.

"It is now half-past-ten. Today is my wife's last day in Baden. You must find the diary, read the entries, form a conclusion on the matter I have commissioned you on, return everything to where it was, and report to me at the opera house at six this evening. For you and you alone, Mr Holmes, I will take time out of rehearsals."

"But had you no scruples about nosing through a woman's dairy for her secrets of the bedroom?" I asked, although, to be fair, I had never known Holmes not to take a case.

Holmes gave another slightly wan smile, but said nothing.

"And had you asked what action Herr Mahler might take if you found the child was not his? You might ruin three lives."

Holmes stared into the distance and did not respond to my question before continuing.

I sat at Frau Mahler's desk and worked away.

After ten minutes I heard the mortice of the lock of the desk turn with a creaking groan and there was the safe before me. My brief had been to crack it, remove the contents, review them, and replace them without leaving any indication of my intervention.

He paused before going on.

Watson, I used every tool I had at my disposal – screwdriver, jemmy, wrench, awl. All in vain. In the background I could hear a little clock on top of the desk ticking away the seconds and minutes. Its sound assumed a greater and greater prominence in my mind as I did my work.

Then completely without warning, the study door swept open and a woman who could only be Frau Mahler stood before me.

"Well, you and my husband made that pretty easy between you," was her first comment.

There was a pause before she continued.

"I was coming down the stairs of the hotel to meet my husband in the lobby when I saw him go up to a man whom my reading of the *Strand Magazine* of which we get every issue told me could only be Mr Sherlock Holmes. You and he, Mr Holmes, then walked straight out of the hotel and into a cab. I went into breakfast and soon afterwards I received a cock-and-bull message from my husband saying he had been detained in Vienna. I had already formed four different hypotheses as to what might be afoot but, knowing his jealousies and suspicions, a break-in to my desk was by far the most likely. And by far the easiest to investigate."

I felt nothing would be served by making any comment and Frau Mahler continued.

"I have had my share of lovers and admirers, Mr Holmes. I am a musician, and the composer Alexander von Zemlinsky was my teacher. He taught me much more than just music. I have an association with Gustav Klimt which means that there has already been more than one Gustav in my life. Architect Walter Grophius has come under my spell. Indeed, Mr, Holmes, it is hard to think of a famous man in our imperial capital by whom I have not yet been wooed at some point. And at twenty-four I do not consider my account closed."

Holmes broke off from his narrative, and, for the only time in our acquaintance, he paused to mop his brow. As my reader may imagine, I was agog to discover what happened next and my friend seemed eager to tell me.

"So, what is to be your plan now, Mr Holmes?" Frau Mahler asked a sudden note of sweetness coming into her voice. "Your commission has been surprised by the one at whom it has been directed."

She paused and her lovely eyes looked deep into mine.

"And yet, dear sir," she went on, "your intellect and your...." she broke off as she sought to bring out the right word from deep within her, "…prowess exceed that of any of the men I have ever…." she broke off again to consider her next word before she contenting herself with the short but ambiguous.…"known."

Her eyes had been full of rage when she first saw me but now they seemed to soften and indeed, as they looked deep into mine, her gaze and mine seemed melded.

Holmes broke off again and said with an outburst of passion the like of which I had never previously seen.

"Good Watson," though in truth his words seemed to be addressed more to himself than to me, "this woman had observed her husband and me in our hotel, she had inferred his disquisition, she had forecast my plan of action. And she had acted on her own and thwarted it. Utterly. No adversary, not even Professor Moriarty of evil memory, or Irene Adler, the only woman with whom Frau Mahler can be compared, had even got close to this. Moriarty lies at the bottom of the Reichenbach Falls while Miss Adler married Geoffrey Norton and took to flight. Frau Mahler trumps them both. What a woman she is!"

Holmes fell silent and stared into the distance as if in a reverie at his recollection of Frau Mahler.

"Your collection of M's is a fine one," said I, referencing what my friend had said at the conclusion of *The Empty House* not for the only time in our acquaintance. If the truth be told, I felt uncomfortable with the very intimate turn that Holmes seemed to be taking and thought referring to past adventures might bring him down to earth. "Moriarty himself is enough to make any letter illustrious, Sebastian Moran twice got close to killing you, there is Morgan the poisoner, Merridew of abominable memory, Mathews, who knocked out your left canine – and now there is the fair Frau Mahler."

"None of the men you mention has the mind, the mystique, the majesty, and the" – Holmes paused to consider what word he should use next and the word he eventually came out with was one I had never heard him use before and never heard him use again outside this confessional – "magic of the latest M, Frau Alma Mahler. It seems only appropriate that, uniquely among the people whom you have mentioned, her name should contain the letter M twice."

He paused.

Normally I think he would have lit his pipe at this point, but so smitten was my friend by Frau Mahler that he abjured even this, and all I could hear were profound almost sobbing intakes of breath.

"In an empty house," he eventually went on, "with any other possible distraction remote, it was impossible not to succumb... yes, good Watson, succumb is the only word that will do... to this magic which she radiated. Fully, unashamedly, without reserve."

There was another long pause for breath.

"I confess, good Watson, at this moment my only regret to the whole turn of events is that the span of time left to me to succumb to Frau Mahler was so limited by my commission to go and see her husband at six o'clock this evening. How does Schiller put it in his *Ode to Joy* which forms the finale of the symphony we heard yesterday evening, 'Deine Zauber binden wieder, was die Mode streng geteilt,' 'Your magic unites once more the things convention keeps well apart.'"

"What did you tell Herr Mahler?" I asked, anxious to move discussions on from topics of an intimate nature where Holmes's confessional had me in considerable discomfort.

But Holmes was still enraptured by his recollections of the day. As if in a dream he quoted, " 'Alle Menschen werden Brüder, wo dein sanfter Flügel weiht'. This was beyond my knowledge of German and Holmes translated. "'All people are as brothers wherever your soft wings bless.' It is indeed hard," Holmes broke off while he considered what to say next, "to imagine anyone writing a better description of what I felt than the great Friedrich Schiller. And the music Beethoven wrote for it is for the gods."

"So what did you tell Herr Mahler?" I repeated for I wanted to make sure I heard the denouement of what my friend had to say.

"It is fortunate indeed," said Holmes, suddenly sounding much more like his normal self, "that my brief included the instruction to make my ingress into Frau Mahler's affairs invisible and do no more than report my findings to Herr Mahler. Accordingly, with Frau Mahler's kind consent, I relocked her desk leaving its safe unpenetrated, and, as I walked the short distance from his quarters to the Opera House, it occurred to me that anything I said to Herr Mahler was impossible to disprove unless he disbelieved me. If that were the case, he would then have to find someone else who made a better job than I had done at breaking into Frau Mahler's safe to read her diaries which I, whom Herr Mahler had described in such flattering terms, had signally failed to do."

He resumed his narrative.

> Herr Mahler was able to see me at the appointed hour and we sat in what he called his offstage office underneath the Opera House's orchestra pit – a room with a desk, a music-stand, a piano and, somewhat to my surprise, for the room was very small, a large and elaborately upholstered couch. The furniture filled every inch of the room.
>
> "You had better take your station on the piano stool," said Mahler. "I have no need for more than one chair in this room and no space for more than one chair either. What have you to say? I must warn you I can only give you a few minutes as our soprano is in urgent need of some further rehearsal and she will join me in here shortly. My instrument is at the ready to help her in any way it can."
>
> "I was able, Herr Mahler," I said, "to make my investigations without leaving any trace of my presence on the desk or the safe…."
>
> "That is nothing less than what I would expect of the greatest mind in Europe," said Mahler with an edge of impatience in his voice which I

suspect he often used to get the best out of his performers.

"…And I found no evidence of any amorous adventures on the part of your wife in February 1901 – other, of course, than those which she evidently enjoyed with you."

Mahler sighed.

"Mr Holmes," replied he at length, "you have given me great comfort. This is a matter that we now have in black and white. I do not think there is anything further for us to say. I must now dedicate myself to getting the most out of the voice of the fair Fräulein Eibenschütz who will be joining me here in a few minutes in this, erm, office. It is striking how much better my performers sing after what may be but a brief rehearsal here."

The maestro sought no further details, and I was in the doorway when he said, "Ah Mr Holmes! Such is the enormity of what you have done and of such a great moment is it to me, I have neglected to reward you for your endeavours."

"The challenge itself was sufficient reward, Maestro," I replied, anxious to get away.

"I assume Dr Watson is still with you."

"He is in Baden where you and I met."

"Then tomorrow night I will get you and him a box here at the Opera to see Mozart's *Così fan tutte*. It is the first production of the work in a hundred…."

I felt I could hear no more of this.

"Holmes, you failed utterly to achieve the objective set you by your client. Instead, you were caught *in flagrante* by the object of your search…"

"She is beyond compare."

"You have lied about your results to your client…"

"Unprovably."

"And you have disported yourself with his wife who was supposed to be the object of your investigations."

Holmes held his counsel on this last point, and I continued.

"And you have now been offered as a reward for your failure a box at the opera."

"No one would commission you," he snorted, much of his normal spirit returning, "to undertake an investigation such as I was asked to perform, and I am not sure I would have succeeded in my brief even if Frau Mahler had not interrupted me. As I have said, no one will be able to disprove what I have said to Herr Mahler. And I am not sure you – or indeed anyone else – would have acted any differently with the lovely Frau Mahler had you had the benefit of seeing her."

I could not be sure – although I confess to having a fairly clear idea – that my winsome companion of the morn had in fact been Frau Mahler for spas are famed for the way people of all types succumb to brief encounters. This lingering uncertainty emboldened me to continue my observations.

"It is as well there is no Institute of Consulting Detectives."

"I remain the world's only consulting detective," interjected Holmes, managing to sound both austere and slightly shifty at the same time, "so there is of course no governing body."

"If there were, you would certainly be drummed out of it for what you have done. If I did what you have done with a patient, I would not be allowed to continue in the medical profession."

"Tomorrow the Vienna Court Opera is staging *Così fan tutte* by Mozart. The first revival of the piece in more than a hundred years. And we have a box at the invitation of Herr Mahler."

That Mozart had written an opera with the title *Così fan tutte* was unknown to me and I was sufficiently curious to ask, "What does *Così fan tutte* mean?"

"It means, 'Women are like that' in Italian," replied Holmes.

"I am not clear that men are much different," I snapped. "And what will we do if Frau Mahler is there to greet us?"

"I am sure I could handle that with aplomb, and I am even surer that Frau Mahler could handle it with aplomb," replied my friend. "Indeed, I would be surprised if the situation had not occurred before."

I was relieved that Holmes failed to ask me why I had used 'we' in my question when, on the knowledge he had, I would have had no reason to be concerned by meeting with Frau Mahler.

The more I thought about the invitation, the less I liked it. Frau Mahler may have had – indeed, as Holmes had suggested, I had no doubt whatever that Frau Mahler had – more than enough experience of such matters to handle a meeting with Holmes, her husband and me with aplomb. But I was not at all sure how Holmes would handle being in the company of a man he (and probably I) had cuckolded, and I was even more unsure that I wanted to be present if my own princess of the morn had indeed been Frau Mahler. From the time Holmes had disclosed his adventure, I had been trying not to calculate the percentage that Holmes and I had not in fact been seduced by the same woman within six hours of each other. Of course, this had the result that I found myself doing nothing else and I never got the probability that there were two different and lovely seductresses working independently of each other in the same place at above ten per cent.

At this point fate intervened as a messenger came into the lobby crying "Telegram für Herrn Holmes!"

My friend rose to receive it.

"It is Mycroft!" he exclaimed. "There is an urgent matter in London requiring my attention – healthy or not, he stresses. We must to England by the night express."

So it was that within a day and half we were back in London, Holmes apparently revivified by his adventure in

Vienna. Ironically, the matter we had been summoned to London for took us back into the Austro-Hungarian Empire and may serve the basis for an account of a future adventure.

It was nine months later that I saw a letter with an Austrian stamp addressed to Holmes at our breakfast table.

He opened it and I saw his eye-brows shoot up.

"Frau Mahler has given birth to a daughter. Let me read you what she has to say."

My reader may imagine that my heartbeat soared as my friend read the letter.

> Dear Mr Holmes,
>
> I thought you should be aware that I have just given birth to a daughter called Anna. She is as beautiful as her sister.
>
> I candidly confess that I have no idea who the father is, but, if you are talking of this matter to your biographer and confessor Dr Watson, you might like to add the detail that, irrespective of who he is, it was a man of great distinction.
>
> Since the encounter you and I had last year, my husband has been attentiveness itself. We have consulted with a local doctor, Dr Sigmund Freud, on the differences that had arisen between us. Dr Freud recommended that my husband allow me to start composing music again and this has greatly eased my anxieties.

Gustav is devotion itself to little Anna, and we are very happy.

Very truly yours,

Alma Mahler

I saw that Gustav Mahler died in 1911 and Alma Mahler subsequently married Walter Grophius, the architect whom she had mentioned in the foregoing, and Franz Werfel, an author, whom she did not.

Anna Mahler became a well-known sculptress and recollection of this as I pen this last paragraph has led me to embargo publication of this work until after her death rather than that of her mother Alma.

Note by Henry Durham, historical advisor to
The Redacted Sherlock Holmes

Future sculptress Anna Mahler is pictured bottom right with her mother, Alma Mahler, and her elder sister, Maria, who was to die in 1907.

The picture of Anna Mahler allows no insight at this distance on whether her father was Gustav Mahler, Sherlock Holmes, or Dr Watson but her dates of 15th of June 1904 to 3rd of June 1988 making it entirely possible that she was sired by Sherlock Holmes or Dr Watson in September 1903 and not by Gustav Mahler.

The Tsar, the Pince-Nez, and the Six-Foot Scowl

My writing has been described as a bringer of comfort to the troubled as my colleague, Mr Sherlock Holmes, finds the solution to a problem presented to him by a petitioner, and this solution, once identified by my friend, is demonstrably logical however mysterious the problem had at first sight appeared. I regret to warn my readers at the outset of the matters I describe in this work, that even though they relate to events they may recognise, the elucidation and resolution of them will lack some of these comforting characteristics as my friend and I were drawn into matters that perhaps reached beyond the limits of where his methods were applicable.

My followers will be aware that there was the long delay in the publication of the events that make up *The Adventure of the Golden Pince-Nez*.

The work's narrative is precisely dated to November 1894 and yet publication was held back until the middle of 1904, so almost ten years later. My published account of events at Yoxley Place near Chatham ended with the self-poisoning of Anna, the female owner of the accoutrement that gave the work its title, and her final words, which she gasped out in an English marked with a heavy Russian accent, were addressed to my friend, as she said. "Here is the packet which will save Alexis. I confide it to your honour and to your love of justice. Take it! You will deliver it at the Russian Embassy."

The packet she referred to contained letters and diaries. These documents, said Anna, whose family-name Holmes and I were destined never to find out, would show that Alexis, a man she described as the friend of her heart and a member of the shadowy Nihilist Brotherhood, had urged fellow members of the Brotherhood to abjure violence at all costs in their attempts to topple the Russian government.

It would be difficult to think of a better way to persuade Holmes to act than to appeal to his honour and love of justice. The version of events that was eventually published ended with him declaring his intention of going to the Russian Embassy forthwith to obtain freedom for Alexis and, as we set off, I recall how my friend's eyes were aflame with righteousness at the prospect of freeing a man unjustly sentenced to forced labour in a salt mine.

So why did the narrative stop where it did? What was the reaction of the Russian authorities to my friend's plea for clemency? And what happened to Alexis afterwards?

The events I describe below explain why the account I gave ended where it did, introduce a whole new plotline the resolution of which Holmes had to explain to me, and provide a conclusion in a way even more unsatisfactory than the already inconclusive ending of *The Golden Pince-Nez* as it finally appeared. In the end my friend was reduced to uttering an aphorism originally coined by his brother, Mycroft, which has itself since gained much wider currency through its use by our current Prime Minister, Mr Churchill, who will doubtless also have heard it from his dealings with Mycroft as the latter works in his role as the government's senior permanent advisor.

It was only on our way to the embassy on that November afternoon that Holmes looked at the documents with which he had been entrusted.

"They are all in Russian!" exclaimed he. "That is a language I do not know, and I do not even follow the Cyrillic alphabet with any facility. I cannot treat with the Russian ambassador without knowing what these documents say in detail. And I will have to have a copy of the Russian version of these letters written out as well as I cannot entrust them to the Russian authorities without having a version of them of my own."

So it was that we turned back to Baker Street and Holmes had to find a transcriber and a translator. With my friend's heavy caseload in 1894, it was into early 1895 before we were finally ready to make our way to the Russian embassy at Chesham Place in Belgravia. Anna's estranged husband, who went by the assumed name of Professor Coram, had refused to disclose to us Alexis's family name and it was only after we had got the translations of the letters that we learned that it was Ivanov or, to give him his full name as we were given it by the translator, Alexis Mikhailovich Ivanov.

We presented ourselves at the Russian embassy where, as was normally the way with such things, my friend's visiting card was sufficient to gain us an immediate audience with the most senior person on site. Thus, we were soon sat before the Russian ambassador, the aged and heavily bewhiskered Baron Egor Egorovich Staal, in a lavishly furnished reception room.

"So, Mr Holmes, you have come to me to present the case of Alexis Mikhailovich Ivanov, who, you say, labours to this day in one of our salt-mines and whom you regard as a political prisoner," said the ambassador in a slow nasal drawl.

"That is so," said my friend. "I cannot tell you how I came into possession of these letters and private diaries, but if you read them will see that Mr Ivanov constantly urged the Nihilist Brotherhood to use peaceful means only. Accordingly, he should not have been sentenced to forced labour in a salt-mine."

"I fear I must disagree with your thesis, Mr Holmes," replied Staal, his deep grey eyes looking steadily back at my friend. "The Nihilists want to overthrow everything that my country holds dear. And to overthrow everything elsewhere too. If you are a citizen of my country and you know where the Nihilists can be found, I would suggest that rather more is required of the citizen than to urge the Nihilists to confine themselves to peaceful means – especially as they are a violent organization which is likely to ignore any plea to that effect."

Holmes was silent and Staal continued.

"On the contrary, it is my view that it is a citizen's duty is to tell the authorities where the Nihilists can be found so that they can be apprehended."

I do not think that Holmes had anticipated this line of argument, and, perhaps sensing he was at an advantage, Staal went on.

"If you, Mr Holmes, knew of a plot against the life of the grandmother of our great Tsar, your Queen Victoria, is it sufficient to urge the plotters not to attempt an assassination? It is surely your duty to help the authorities to bring the plotters into custody so that their plot can be thwarted, and so that appropriate retributive punishment can follow."

Again, my friend was struck dumb, and Staal carried on uninterrupted.

"For my own part, Mr Holmes, I must confess that I find some of your activities as described by your friend, Dr Watson, here somewhat disturbing. While your detective work, it hardly needs to be said, is beyond reproach, in *The Blue Carbuncle* you free a thief who has tried to frame someone else for his crime. And *in The Boscombe Valley Mystery*, you free a man who is both a murderer and a highwayman. Quite apart from the question of your judgment, you are, if I may say so, taking on rather more responsibility than is appropriate for an ordinary individual. You are deciding things that it is for a higher power to do."

"But a man who has no knowledge of specific actions to be taken by another cannot be detained indefinitely based on those actions that were taken. It does not take any sort of higher power to decide that," objected my friend.

The ambassador sighed.

"You are here, Mr Holmes, before the law and I am merely its first gate-keeper. Even if you pass to its second gate, you will be faced by another gate-keeper, who is more powerful than I, and then a third, who is more powerful still." He paused and glanced down at the documents on the desk before him. "I cannot guarantee that you will get any further with these people either. I fear I will not be the person to make any sort of decision on this matter."

"But you hold the title of the Russian ambassador to this country."

Another sigh.

"Nevertheless, your disquisition must go to a higher authority in my country's hierarchy if it is to be considered."

"So do I have your undertaking that you will raise the matter at a more senior level?"

"Perhaps you should return when I have had more time to consider it in detail."

Over the next few months, we made weary return after weary return to see Baron Staal at the Russian Embassy. My friend was indefatigable in his efforts – "Thrice armed is he that hath his quarrel just," he quoted to me after another rebuff – but it was to no avail. It was striking that even though we never made an appointment to see him, for all that we were always returning with the same petition, we were each time put before the Baron when we arrived. At one point Holmes asked him why he was always available to see us and got the reply, "For a person such as you, Mr Holmes, the only person suitable to see you in London is my country's ambassador for all that my powers are so limited."

In the end Holmes took to sending letters directly to the Tsar in St Petersburg. And yet these were always forwarded to Staal in London. "I will of course continue to see you Mr Holmes," he said to us at one point, "despite your attempts to bypass me. But you should be aware that I do so only in order that you can be sure that you have left no stone unturned in your endeavours."

I have no idea how long this might have gone on for but in February 1897 a letter arrived in an envelope with a large and heavily embossed coat of arms on it. My friend opened it over his after-breakfast pipe.

"Well, well," commented he jovially, "we will be hobnobbing with an emperor."

I looked questioningly at him.

"We have been asked to go to St. Petersburg to meet Tsar Nicholas II."

"Does the invitation specify the reason why we are being asked to go to St. Petersburg?"

"I cannot believe it is unconnected with our efforts on behalf of Ivanov although that is not stated in the letter. At last, we advance."

I will not detain my reader with the details of the journey by train from London via Paris and Berlin to the Russian capital via a change of trains at Brest-Litovsk to accommodate the wider track gauge used on Russian railways. At the final station, Moskovske Voxhall, our proffered handshakes were met with an exuberant kiss and bear-hug by the ebullient Russian Foreign Minister,

Mikhael Artemyevich Muravyov. The air was filled with the familiar smell of steam and hot metal from the locomotive as the Russian dignitary said, "The second part of the name of this station is derived from your Vauxhall Station in London. You will find much here that is familiar to you, and yet there is still so much we can learn from you English. Not just in railway engineering but in principles of governance and justice."

"I take it from that remark," said Holmes, "that you refer to our pursuit of justice for Alexis Ivanov."

"You will be tired by your long journey, and I will take to your hotel," replied the minister sounding slightly evasive.

"Justice delayed is justice denied," objected Holmes to what I am sure he regarded as a rebuff from minister.

"You will be tired by your long journey, and I will take to your hotel," repeated Muravyov, and this time the sentence was said with an edge in the tone which made it clear that further counter-argument would cause more problems than it would solve.

Over the next few days, Holmes and I were treated like royalty as we were taken round the sights of St. Petersburg. Muravyov accompanied us everywhere we went. "I am the only person of my level who can host dignitaries such as yourselves. Someone just up from the country would not get to see a foreign minister," he said to us at one point, but whenever Holmes sought to press the case of Ivanov, Muravyov would say, without referring to Ivanov's case at all, that everything had been arranged in accordance with a timetable which was under the control of people more senior than himself.

It was by my diary the 28th of March before matters advanced.

"Gentlemen," Muravyov said as we sat over a lunch at which Holmes had again sought to raise Ivanov's case and had again been rebuffed, "this afternoon I would like to demonstrate to you how Russian culture is alive and abundant. We are going to a Russian Symphony Concert at the Dom Muski. This is a series of concerts that specialises in new Russian music."

As we arrived at the Dom Muski, a messenger dashed up to us and handed to Muravyov an envelope. He opened it and uttered what from the tone used sounded like some sort of imprecation. "I fear gentlemen, I have been called away on urgent business. But the music is all orchestral, so you won't need to know any of the Russian language to enjoy it. I will arrange for you to be picked up at the concert's end."

I believe we were the sole non-Russians in the hall as the audience gathered in the auditorium.

My published writings refer to Holmes playing Mendelssohn lieder or songs on the violin and to hearing Pablo de Sarasate play his violin – German music rather than Italian or French as Holmes pointed out – at St. James's Hall. We also went to Wagner and Meyerbeer at Covent Garden. But such musical feasts were always at Holmes's instigation and there were not many evenings that I went to a concert on my own. I certainly had no idea of what to expect from a concert of new Russian music. And from the program which I had bought as a souvenir I got was no help at all as it was all in the Cyrillic script.

There was a burst of applause as the conductor came on and took his bow before the soberly attired audience and the music started with a dramatic gesture. The first half had a short piece followed by a longer piece and we remained in our seats at the interval. As the second half got under way, I was startled to note fumes of alcohol coming from I knew not where. The audience had come back from what I assumed were interval drinks, but I had not noticed any untoward behaviour from them and in the end I focused my attention on the music which was even more raucous than the pieces that had made up the first part of the concert. Even to my unmusical ears, the brass sounded discordant and over-emphasised, and the music itself bereft of memorable tunes. I think the conductor too was dissatisfied and between movements he held onto the railing behind his rostrum and sipped at a glass propped on it at the end of the first movement.

Half an hour later, and not before a young man seated at the end of our row had made a noisy break for the exit, the second half of the concert came to an end. As the lights came on, the conductor bowed to the audience although I noted he was holding tight onto the podium's railing as he did so. As I looked around at the banks of bare seats in the auditorium, I saw that the young man I had seen was not the only person who had left.

"Spirited music," said Holmes drily as some desultory applause broke out from those members of the audience who had remained, and we rose to head to the foyer. As we got there a messenger ran up to us with the same urgency as the messenger who had approached Muravyov and said in highly accented English, "The Tsar will see you this instant at the Imperial Palace."

A carriage was waiting for us outside the concert-hall and whisked us to the Tsar's imposing pistachio-coloured residence. Double door after double door spanning long carpeted corridors were swung open to us, and soon we were being greeted by the bearded, thirty-year-old Russian leader in his office, he seated at one end of a table the length of a cricket-pitch, and we at the other.

"It feels to me, Mr Holmes," began Nicholas II in a polished English, "that I was fashioned simply to meet you."

"I am here to present the case of Alexis Mikhailovich Ivanov," said Holmes.

"I am threatened on all sides by hostile elements," replied the Tsar, paying no apparent heed to the words of my friend, "and it is very difficult to know the best way of dealing with them. There are Bolsheviks, Anarchists, Nihilists, Socialists, Social Democrats, as well as the Russian Orthodox Church. If I make concessions to any of them, they will threaten our Russian way of life. The balance of forces we have now is the only thing that keeps us from anarchy which is why I strive to maintain things as they are. During the last months there have been voices calling for these forces to participate in the government of the country. I want everyone to know that I will devote all my strength to maintain, for the good of the whole nation, the principle of absolute autocracy, as firmly and as strongly as did my late lamented father who was leader of my people before me."

"Pray continue," said Holmes, I think unclear, as I was, where the Tsar's disquisition was leading.

"I am looking to give an example to these hostile elements of a man whom they can look up to. A man who can be a model for those who would wish to overthrow the status quo. A man of honour who is a free-thinker but who poses no threat to me."

Holmes, as I saw more than once during our long association, was accessible on the side of flattery, and at the Tsar's words my friend rose slightly in chair, but he confined himself to murmuring his familiar refrain of, "Pray continue."

"The Nihilist, Alexis Mikhailovich Ivanov, fits the category," said the Tsar mildly.

I saw Holmes sink back a little in his chair and the Tsar continued.

"You, Mr Holmes, have been advocating Ivanov's freedom."

"That is so," replied Holmes, still looking a little crestfallen. "I have been making it clear to your representatives both here in St. Petersburg and in London, that Ivanov was pleading with the Nihilist Brotherhood to avoid violence, and so should not be subject to incarceration."

"But he knew who they were and so he believed in their objectives even if he deplored their methods. He was a fellow traveller."

"I have explained his role in which he sought to moderate the actions of the Nihilist Brotherhood. I have reason to believe he is now doing hard labour in a Siberian salt-mine for his pains."

"I imagine you know about him because of some event that is likely to form the basis of one of the…" – he paused to consider his next word.., "popular…" the word hung in the air before the Tsar continued – "works that your companion here produces."

"I fear," said Holmes with a slightly weary sigh, "that the events which led me to take an interest in Ivanov are sufficiently grotesque to appeal to my colleague's undiscerning public. They have a taste for the romanticised version of events with their meretricious finales that he produces whereas as to me it is the logic of my approach to solving a case which should be showcased. I therefore fear that it is likely that he will produce one of his pamphlets on it although he always offers me the opportunity to embargo the publication of any work or make modifications to it. But I am here to obtain justice for Alexis Ivanov not to discuss how my friend chooses to present the events that brought us here."

"Very well. Then I think I can give you a fitting conclusion to your friend's work."

"Pray continue," said my friend again.

"I have decided to release Ivanov for the reasons you state. He called for peaceful methods to be used, and he has served his time. That will enable Dr Watson to end his account of events with an ending that will be ostensibly happy."

"And where is Ivanov now?"

"He is in the room next door."

"I should like to see him being released."

"I am happy to say that you shall see more than that, Mr Holmes. You will see him rehabilitated. He is admirably suited to being a free-thinker who does not threaten me."

"Could I ask you to explain what you are proposing?"

The Tsar picked up a piece of paper from the table in front of him.

"Tomorrow's *Government Gazette*, the main newspaper of my country, will have the following article. I will translate for you.

> Many people (began the Tsar) faced with a lengthy and deserved sentence in a salt mine for political subversion, would have allowed themselves to become embittered. But reformed Nihilist, Alexis Mikhailovich Ivanov, decided to use his sentence to seek redemption. He laboured diligently at his work and never ceased to make remarks to his fellow-prisoners praising the Tsar's mercy for not having him hanged.

43

As a result of Ivanov's behaviour, the Tsar has issued a special decree. Ivanov has been freed, and he will return to his family. Ivanov himself has said he will use the talents and energies he previously squandered on Nilhilism for praising the rule of the Tsar.

The Tsar's attention was drawn to Ivanov's case by the visit to Moscow from London of the famous detective, Mr Sherlock Holmes.

For his part Mr Holmes has commented, 'I am grateful that the Tsar has found it in his heart to pardon a sinner, just as in my own small way I hope my work makes humanity my beneficiary.

At this moment, a door opened and a man in shackles, heavily bearded, suffused with pustules, and gaunt to the point of starvation, was brought in. He proceeded to prostrate himself before the Tsar and mumbled as he did so. I heard a word which sounded something like "tsar-batiushka" repeated over and over again.

"It means dear Tsar and is a term of adoration," explained the Tsar looking up at us and completely ignoring Ivanov. "He is referring to me and adoration is appropriate as I am granting him his freedom as it is in my gift to do." The Tsar broke off and barked something that sounded like, "Tischina Ivanov!" at his suppliant who was still abasing himself and repeating "tsar-batiushka." Ivanov appeared not to notice what the Tsar was saying, and the Tsar again barked out, "Tischina Ivanov!"

It was only after "Tischina Ivanov!" had been repeated a second time and then a third time and the tsar had prodded Ivanov with his toe that the latter at last fell silent.

"And you think the recounting of the release of a prisoner in this condition and under these circumstances would be an appropriate ending to a work by my colleague?" asked Holmes.

"That is my judgment, Mr Holmes. And my judgment will have your approbation. The approbation of Mr Sherlock Holmes – one of the minds of this age. And if it does not, then the prisoner will not be freed. For all that, I doubt very much that Ivanov will live for much longer. His release will demonstrate to the world that I am merciful, and his pitiful condition will act as a warning to those who would oppose me."

"I confess I do not know how Dr Watson will handle this, and I do not wish to be associated with this. It is not the bestowal of justice."

"It is justice, Mr Holmes. It is the form of justice that I dispense, and it is Russian justice." The Tsar's gaze flickered between the two of us. "This form of justice is not final because it is right. It is right because it is final."

There was a long pause, and it was the Tsar who spoke next seemingly as a piece of *obiter dicta* or side remark. "Unless of course I subsequently decide to consider the matter differently."

"And you would like my friend to describe the events we have seen here accurately?" asked Holmes.

"I would like the way your friend presents me to reflect the way I am presented in the newspaper article. Masterful but merciful."

The Tsar had another thought and added.

"Think of the story of Job. Job is put to the test by God. His children are slain, his wealth is destroyed, and his health is ruined. Yet he remains respectful of God. That is the way I see myself."

"You see yourself as Job?" I asked, slightly puzzled.

Nicolai looked down at Ivanov, then at Holmes. "You often complain that Dr Watson does not present things as they are. But in his description of his own intellectual limitations, he is accurate." He fixed me with a gaze. "Does my prisoner not call me holy, Dr Watson? Is it not he who is covered in boils? Whom do you think I see myself as in the story of Job?"

"So to summarise," said Holmes, "if my friend portrays you as a godly figure dispensing justice, you will turn Ivanov free?"

"That is so," replied the Tsar airily, "although, obviously, any future consorting with Nihilists on Ivanov's part, will see him hanged without further ado."

"If you see yourself in the way that you do, why do you seek my approbation?"

"No one ever was worse off from having the approbation of Mr Sherlock Holmes."

"I don't like it Holmes," I interjected. "To conclude a narrative with a broken man being freed on condition that I put a particular construction on events and that I portray you as approving it, is not something I am comfortable with." I turned to the Tsar and added, "You will understand, that a work by me which may have diplomatic ramifications will have to be cleared by the British Foreign Office before it can be released to the public."

The Tsar shrugged.

"Then we will see what your Foreign Office has to say. I will have the events of this evening we – no, Dr Watson now sets down cabled to London this evening. But what I am asking you to do will show me to be a strong man to my people. And in St. Petersburg they will see Ivanov as a broken man and realise I am not to be trifled with. And my act of mercy will improve my reputation overseas. If you agree to what I propose, the prisoner will go free. If not, he will be sent back to Siberia."

At the mention of the word "Siberia" which I subsequently confirmed is called Sibir' in Russian and so must have been recognisable to him, Ivanov broke into uncontrollable sobs, and this forced my hand.

I will not weary my reader with the toing and froing that went on across the absurd length of the table between Holmes and me at one end and the Tsar at the other but in the end I felt I had no choice except to accede to the Tsar's request. For his part the Tsar insisted I write a version of the above events in a form suitable to the ending of *The Golden Pince-Nez* on the spot. When I said I had finished, he walked the length of the table and looked over my shoulder to ask for some final amendments to the text. Only when he was fully satisfied with what I had written, were we allowed to leave the palace. The one concession we wrung from him was that Ivanov would be placed under house arrest with his family and was not returned to Siberia pending a response from London.

Holmes was, I think, as shaken by events as I, and we exchanged not a word as we returned to our hotel, packed our few possessions, and made our way to the station to make the long journey back to London, accompanied as ever by Muravyov.

When we eventually entered the flat at Baker Street, it was to find Mycroft Holmes (whom I will normally refer to as Mycroft to avoid confusion with his brother) pacing the floor of our sitting-room.

"What have you allowed yourself to get into, Sherlock? Here am I in London trying to negotiate a top-secret treaty with the French, and you let yourself get mixed up with the Russians."

I have elsewhere described my friend's knowledge of politics as feeble, but this development was news to me too even though I pride myself on remaining abreast of political developments.

"But what has a top-secret treaty with France got to do with our recent sojourn in Russia?" I asked.

"It is the *entente cordiale*. Have you not heard of it?"

I could see Holmes – not unexpectedly – looking blank, but I was similarly at a loss.

"I thought everyone had heard of it. We are seeking an understanding with the French on a number of colonial matters," Mycroft said, and he continued cryptically, "It is to get one over the Germans and the Austrians."

"I repeat, what has that got to do with our time in Russia?" I asked.

"France is in alliance with the Russians so, to get the French to sign the treaty we need to square the Russians. And we need to get the treaty past British public opinion which has fresh memories of wars with the French and the Russians and none of any enmity with Germany which has only been in existence for the last thirty years, but which is already showing a bellicosity that requires curbing, and which is sidling up to the Austrians."

"But what is all that to us? We have our Empire and no significant interests in Europe so why do we need an alliance with the French and the Russians to get one over the Germans and the Austrians?"

Mycroft stared at me.

"Well, naturally so that we can continue to have no significant interests in Europe. If we are in alliance with the French and the Russians, and the Germans and the Austrians have a balancing alliance of their own, then Europe is as shackled as your friend Ivanov, and will leave us alone to focus on building our global empire where the opportunities for territorial aggrandizement are more succulent. But having my brother, who through your writings has a reputation for sound judgment quite at variance from what I know of him, endorse the behaviour of the Tsar as he toys with a broken man, will be quite sufficient to cause questions to be raised in Parliament about the desirability of this treaty. The people's representatives have an understanding of *Realpolitik* that is as uninformed as that of brother Sherlock here."

"But surely no one in this country would be interested in the fate of an obscure Russian political prisoner."

"Not unless his fate were given currency by your...," Mycroft broke off to consider the *mot juste*... "popular writings, dear Doctor. We may now get demonstrators outside the Russian Embassy, and I am sure Scotland Yard will be too supine to do anything about it. They are selective about which demonstrations they take measures about and those they do not, and I have a clear idea about how they will police one outside the Russian Embassy. Several years' diplomatic work will lie in ruins."

We were at an impasse and in the end Mycroft brought discussions to a close by saying, "I suppose I will have to sort this matter out with the Russians myself," before stalking out with a parting shot of, "Do not either of you meddle with things you do not understand. Really, dealing with anything to do with Russia is like dealing with a riddle wrapped in a mystery inside an enigma."

Over the next few weeks and months Mycroft was a regular visitor to our quarters as he checked with us on what had been agreed with the Tsar and what not. My nerves were quite put on edge as were those of Holmes especially as this coincided with a lull in his case-load. In the end one afternoon in mid-November my friend said, "Well, good Watson, I have no case in prospect. Indeed, the only prospect I have is that of another visit from my brother to harangue me which is something I would prefer to avoid. What say you to a ramble through London?"

For the next three hours we braved the foggy streets and returned just as it was getting dark for the buttons to say, "There was a caller for you gentlemen. Wouldn't say what he wanted or who he was and left in a huff."

"I could do with a case," commented Holmes, as we went up the stairs to the flat. "And if the boy in buttons cannot recognise our caller, then he cannot have been Mycroft who seems to think he has a season-ticket to call here even if this caller seems to have left in a huff just as my brother always does."

As the buttons had said, our caller had gone but lying on the table was a pair of gloves.

"Other than perhaps a watch, a pipe, or bootlaces, nothing tells one more about an individual than a pair of gloves," said Holmes thoughtfully, as he picked them up. I had learned before not to query my friend's confidence in making deductions from the most trivial impedimenta and I sat back to listen to what he had to say.

Normally my friend tossed off his deductions in a matter of seconds but this time he took out a magnifying glass and examined each glove minutely.

"Generally," he said at length, "such examinations are interesting but trivial. But I would not characterise what I see here as trivial for it is clear we are dealing with a remarkable individual."

I knew better than to interrupt my friend at moments such as these and held my counsel.

He continued.

"These are gloves of the highest quality. They are made of marmot skin, and I would not seek to put an estimate on what our visitor paid for them as they are hand-made. And they are obviously of great significance to our caller as he has had his initials, PCB, stitched into them."

He held them up to the light and extended the thumb.

"And then look at their size. They span quite half a thumb's length more than mine. Our petitioner must be a giant – well over six-foot. And he must seek to protect his hands with these gloves which he must value highly, or he would not have had them initialled, and yet he is pre-occupied enough to have left them here."

"So what do you think he does for a living?"

"It is hard to imagine him as anything other than a pianist as with hands this size he can span an octave and a half on the keyboard."

"But these gloves would fit anyone of a large stature."

"But it would be a small number of people who would take such pains to protect their hands by having gloves of this quality."

"You identified that Miss Violet Smith was a pianist by spatulate finger ends and a spirituality of the face. Here you…"

"If I consult my files, good doctor," interrupted Holmes and going to his shelves, "I will identify our caller by searching for a pianist with the initials PCB."

But before he could complete his scrutiny of the bulky file, the bell downstairs had tolled, there were heavy footsteps on the stairs and our door had opened to a man of giant stature.

"Mr Holmes, I called earlier and in my distraction, I left...."

"Not a word more, dear sir," said Holmes standing at the shelves. "I have already identified that you are a pianist with the initials PCB."

"My name," our interlocutor replied, "is Sergei Vasilyevich Rachmaninov. In Russia, in identifying a person by his initials, the family name normally comes first, followed by the name given to a person by his family, and then the patronymic. And the letters are Cyrillic. Thus, what to you looks like the initials of someone with the initials PCB in fact refers to someone who is referred to in Russian as Rachmaninov Sergei Vasilyevich or here in western Europe as Sergei Vasilyevich Rachmaninov. So please do not waste your time looking for a pianist whose initials are PCB for in Russian R is written P, S is written C, and V is written B."

I cannot ever remember a deduction by Holmes being so readily dismissed.

"I am, however, a pianist," continued our visitor, a man in his mid-twenties whose countenance and features were of saturnine darkness, and who, we subsequently learned, had acquired the sobriquet of the Six-Foot Scowl. "The size of my hands as indicated by my gloves is proof enough of what I do, and the skill used in their making should tell you that I am good at it. No one has ever been able to scale the keyboard in the way that I can, and you might even have been able to work out my identity from that distinguishing feature. I would be grateful if you would now return to me my gloves."

"At least I was right on your profession, Mr Rachmaninov," said my friend, handing the gloves over.

"That is so," said our visitor, his gloomy features unchanged and his tone still gruff, "although I must admit I would have expected something rather more insightful from Mr Sherlock Holmes."

"And what brings you here?" asked Holmes in the soothing tone he could adopt so easily when it suited him.

"Eight months ago," began our visitor, a much less combative note entering his voice, "I had my first symphony premiered in St. Petersburg. The conductor was a man called Alexander Konstantinovic Glazunov, who is also a composer. Whether it was through poor work on my part or poor conducting on his, the performance was a catastrophe."

"Was that a concert in March of this year?" asked I.

I went to the diary that I kept intermittently when I shared quarters with Holmes mainly, I confess, to note down source materials for the versions of our adventures that I published. "It was on the 28th of March that the concert took place," I added.

For the first time, a smile crossed our visitor's face, and he turned to face me.

"I am unsurprised to find you so quick on the uptake, Dr Watson. Of course, we have a different calendar in Russia so for us it was the 15th of March but what you say was correct. But how was it that you knew about the concert?"

After I had given a heavily circumscribed explanation of our presence at the concert at the Dom, Rachmaninov continued.

"I fled from the hall."

"So, it was you I saw dashing for the exit," I commented.

"After the concert," continued our visitor, ignoring my interjection, "a leading musical writer, Cesar Antonovich Cui said my work would delight the inhabitants of hell, and that it sounded like the description of the ten plagues of Egypt."

"That seems a somewhat vituperative response," said Holmes.

"Does your friend not report you as saying that everything should be presented as it is, Mr Holmes?" said our visitor, his harsh tone returning. "I am sure Cui was presenting matters as he heard them."

"And what is your own opinion of your work?" asked Holmes hastily.

"I do not know what to think about it. Since that day in March, I have been unable to write anything at all. I have been in the profoundest melancholy, and I cannot even face sitting over a piece of music manuscript paper. I have sought the help of a Muscovite hypnotist, Nikolai Vladimirovich Dahl, to try to discover my creative muse. He has put me into a numerous trances and said over and over again, 'You will begin to write a concerto ... You will work with great facility ... The concerto will be of an excellent quality.' I listen to what he says, but it is to no avail."

"I see," said Holmes at last. "And what would you like me to do?"

"I did not come here to seek advice from you, Mr Holmes."

My friend confined his response to raising his eyebrows and Rachmaninov continued.

"I have had the opportunity of reading the works of your colleague Dr Watson here and in *The Six Napoleons* he makes some fascinating remarks about the *idée fixe*. He says there are no limits to the possibilities of it and adds that it may be trifling in character, and accompanied by complete sanity in every other way apart from where the idea is fixed."

"What of it?" I asked slightly nervously.

"And in another case you display a knowledge of recent writings on nervous lesions. I feel the block on my writing of music is like an *idée fixe*, for I remain sane in every other way. If you can describe an *idée fixe* in the way you have, you are also the person who can help me get rid of it."

"I have been a military doctor," I said cautiously, "And for a few years I was a general practitioner. I had a practice in

Paddington and then in Kensington. I confess I feel you may be better off seeing an expert on diseases of the nervous system of whom there are many in London."

"I fear I have become tired of listening to people claiming to be experts. You, Dr Watson, are a man of the world and it is your word I would wish to hear."

By late 1897 it was already more than three years since I had practised medicine, but I thought I might as well start at the beginning if Rachmaninov really wanted to consult with me rather than with Holmes.

"Very well then, Mr Rachmaninov." In retrospect, I might have sought to put my patient at his ease by addressing him as Vasilyevich, but my patient let it pass. "Do you smoke?"

"I do. I smoke Russian cigarettes, Dr Watson. I have been unable to break the habit I learnt in St. Petersburg. I find the sort of cigarette common elsewhere does not have the same effect."

"What is a Russian cigarette?" asked I, wondering how it might differ from the cigarettes that I myself smoked.

For answer our visitor took out a cardboard tube and a piece of cigarette paper which he filled with tobacco. He put the paper into the tube and lit up. "I find this most soothing," he said. "It is my only comfort at this time when I have become obsessed with the idea I cannot compose. I fear your western style cigarettes do not have the same impact on my mood."

I had never seen a cigarette of this type before – a *papirosi*, our visitor told us – but confined myself to commenting, "I am sure that regular use of tobacco is to be recommended in your current state, and it may even be wise that you smoke it unfiltered to get its full benefit as this type of cigarette will enable you to do. Do you drink?" I asked.

"No more than is normal in my country," came the guarded reply.

"I have an idea your conductor was drunk when he conducted your symphony," chimed in Holmes, who had sat in silence as I sought to learn more about my patient. "That may explain why it failed to have the reception you had hoped for."

Our visitor shrugged. "You are expressing the same opinion of the conductor that my cousin did, Mr Holmes. But I think Maestro Glazunov, who is an experienced and successful director of music, was much as he always is, and I do not attribute any failure of my music to a state of intoxication on his part."

"So what do you attribute it to?"

Rachmaninov shrugged again. "I have not given the matter any thought. I am merely eager to recover my ability to write music no matter what reception it gets. That is why I am here to see Dr Watson. The failure of my first symphony is of no moment to me now as I do not propose to allow it to be performed again."

Over the next few weeks our little sitting-room saw only two visitors as the lull in my friend's caseload continued.

Some days it would be Mycroft Holmes who was trying to find a way to square the circle of getting the treatment of

Ivanov by the Tsar presented in a way which would not cause protests in this country while satisfying the demands of the Tsar's ego in such a way as to push the treaty to signature. In fact, I think Mycroft only came to Baker Street to give vent to the frustration he felt, for, rather than in any way consulting with his brother, he filled the air with words such as "callow," "over-tasked," and "immature."

On other days it was Sergei Rachmaninov, who, despite his gruff manner, hung onto my every word for all that I felt that I was over-tasked to solve his composer's block. I tried to modify the composer's regimen of tobacco and alcohol consumption both up and down to see if that had any effect. I went for long walks with him, to try to improve his sleep pattern and I tried a number of preparations of various origins on him. I even resorted to the therapy that Rachmaninov's Russian hypnotist, Dahl, had tried and at my bidding Rachmaninov repeated the mantra of, "You will begin to write a concerto ... You will work with great facility ... The concerto will be of an excellent quality." But with no better results. Sometimes Rachmaninov would say in tones ranging from a whimper to an asseveration, "I have lost my muse forever," and at other times would wail, "I have music in my head, but I have no idea of how to bring it out."

Holmes, for all that it sounds unorthodox, attended my consultations with Rachmaninov. The composer had no objections to this, commenting accurately that I had attended many of my friend's most sensitive consultations. At one point my friend interrupted my consultation with the composer and suggested Rachmaninov try some of the seven per cent solution of cocaine he himself had previously used. To my consternation Holmes rose and got the familiar bottle down from the shelf where it had for years been gathering dust.

"Friend Watson here," he said, warming to his theme and gesturing vaguely with his pipe towards me, "refers in his works to my drug-addled dreams. For my own part, I have always found cocaine a remarkable stimulant to thought. The only reason why I stopped using it was because my case-load became sufficiently stimulating in its own right for me not to need it any more for all that Watson tries to take the credit for weaning me off it."

I could see the composer havering on my friend's well-intentioned offer.

"I do not know," said Rachmaninov at last, "whether my nerves, which are still shaken by my continued inability to do something that I had been doing since I was twelve, would be strong enough to take something like that."

I think the composer's rejection of Holmes's offer disappointed my friend. At any rate, he shrugged took himself to one side of us, and buried himself in a newspaper, but he was soon to interrupt us again.

"I see from *The Times* that there is a concert at St James's Hall this lunchtime where some of your music is being played, Mr Rachmaninov. What say you if we went and listened to that?"

We walked down Baker Street to Oxford Street, headed east until we got to Regent Street and then south to the corner of that road with Piccadilly.

"I would wish to listen without anyone other than the three of us knowing I am here," said the composer, so we went in and bought tickets for seats at the back of the hall. The concert contained music by Liszt and Chopin and the first half ended with a piece by my patient. I had not yet heard any music by him, and I was struck by its ringing beauty, and, as a smile ghosted over Holmes's face, I could see that he was impressed too. At the piece's conclusion the audience burst into loud and prolonged applause.

"It is my most famous work," said the composer in his customary guttural tones. "It is my Prelude in C sharp minor."

"Why is it at the end of the first half of the concert if it is a Prelude?" I asked.

Rachmaninov shrugged.

"That is the name of the piece. Bach's Preludes precede a fugue in the same key. My preludes precede nothing, but I plan to write one in every key just as Bach did. Many, many times I wish I had not written the piece you have just heard at all. Its success means that nothing else I have written is ever listened to."

After the second half we left the hall and at Holmes's suggestion we continued our walk, heading eastwards along Shaftesbury Avenue, north along Charing Cross Road, and continued eastwards again along High Holborn.

I would estimate Rachmaninov as being six foot six inches and Holmes as six foot and, with their long strides, we were soon in a residential quarter east of the Bank. Some children, off school for the Christmas holidays, were playing on the pavement and singing Christmas carols.

"We, of course, celebrate Christmas on your sixth of January in Russia so our children are at school at this time," said the composer, as we skirted them. By now we were close to St. Mary le Bow Church which started to chime the hour. As it did so, the children switched from singing carols to singing *Oranges and Lemons* ending with 'I do not know, says the Great Bell of Bow' at the end."

"That's it!" exclaimed the composer and, to my bewilderment, he bolted from the scene.

There seemed to me no point in continuing our walk in the absence of the composer and so Holmes and I repaired to Baker Street where we were relieved to find no Mycroft pacing our floor. I have no reason to think that it was anything other than chance that at this point my friend's caseload picked up and, in spite of further visits from Mycroft, I thought little more of the matter.

It was in 1901 that I received a letter from Rachmaninov from whom I had not heard since he abandoned Holmes and me at St. Mary le Bow Church.

> Dear Dr Watson,
>
> Your care has enabled me to take up my pen once more and yesterday my second Piano Concerto, my first work since my first symphony, has been premiered here in St. Petersburg. I am happy to say that it received huge applause.

It opens with the sound of the piano imitating a tolling bell and the bottom note of the peal is an F which is the same note as the bottom of the toll of the church at St. Mary le Bow which is where our last consultation ended. Hearing that peal was what inspired me to write this concerto which the critics have said is indeed of excellent quality. That this bottom note concludes the phrase "I do not know," seems appropriate as I did not know how to continue before I submitted myself to your care. But now I have been able to find a way.

I would like to dedicate my new work to you as an expression of my gratitude towards you and would welcome your permission to do this.

I remain, yours sincerely,

Sergei Vasilyevich Rachmaninov

I read the letter to Holmes who chuckled and said, "Ah, good Watson, so you are still none the wis…" but before he could complete what he had to say we heard heavy footsteps on the stairs, the door burst open, and Mycroft stood before us looking as close to being agitated as I have ever seen him.

"We have progressed!" he cried, "Ivanov has died, and as a result the Tsar has entirely lost interest in him. Quick, Dr Watson. Here is a pen. Draft an ending to *The Golden Pince-Nez* cutting it off at the point where you and my brother make to go to the Russian embassy. Your readers need never know the shenanigans that followed or that Ivanov died before he could be freed from confinement.

The Tsar has conceded there is no point making anything out of the case of Ivanov now. If you conclude your account at the point where my brother states his intention of going to the embassy, we will look as though we have acted in the right way, and there will be no popular reaction against the Russians in this country, when the matter comes out in the press."

"So we have to wait for an innocent man to die in custody before we can progress on your treaty?" asked Holmes.

"This is no time for minor scruples, dear brother. Ivanov's fate is none of my doing. This diplomatic exercise is like a complex mechanism falling into place without any moving parts being visible to the outsider."

"Or of a trapdoor opening as an innocent man is despatched from a gallows."

Mycroft ignored his brother's remark. And although my reader may understand my misgivings at censoring the conclusion of the account of events, I undertook to do so partly to avoid a diplomatic embarrassment but partly also to forfend further visits from Mycroft and so to protect the mental health of my friend.

Rather as the Tsar had done in St. Petersburg, Mycroft hung over my shoulder to check that I had penned the paragraphs as he wanted. I was subsequently to learn that the negotiations over the *entente cordiale* had been going on since 1881 so it should not surprise my reader to learn that although Mycroft thought his treaty negotiations were at last at an end in 1901, the terms of it were not finally agreed until the middle of 1904. It hardly needs pointing out that the announcement of the *entente* agreement coincided with the final publication of *The Golden Pince-Nez*.

Mycroft was almost out of the door before I thought to ask him about the request from Rachmaninov to dedicate his new concerto to me.

He asked for more detail and, the more I gave, the more a look of alarm crossed his face before he said, "The more the world knows about the murder in Chatham and the less it knows about anything else you may have had to do with Russia, the better. I am allowing you to publish your version of events at Yoxley Place only because it is better that there is a published version of events involving a solved death even though the killer has herself died. If the Yoxley case is left unexplained, it will cause even more questions to be asked about the efficacy of the police than are asked already. You must, Dr Watson, write to your client that he must look elsewhere for a dedicatee. Perhaps he might dedicate his work to his hypnotist who is safely confined to Russia and, given the way the Tsar administers justice, will not look to meddle in things he does not understand."

And then at last, Mycroft departed, leaving Holmes and me sitting in our chairs at either side of the hearth.

I have described Mycroft's visit in only a few hundred words, but my reader will understand that the matters treated took over two hours to be resolved and I had puffed at my pipe for several minutes before it occurred to me to ask my friend what he had been about to say before his brother had arrived.

"So, good Watson," came the reply, "you, like Mr Rachmaninov, are failing to see how it was I who resolved his composer's block."

Holmes took my silence as his cue to continue.

"I saw all your attempts to change Rachmaninov's regimen, but it seemed to me they ignored the fact that the composer frequently said he could compose if only something would release the flood of ideas."

"But he also said that he could never compose again."

"That is so, but I thought if the music were truly still inside him, then it would only require the right stimulus, rather than a change in his regimen to bring it out. I initially suggested the cocaine as such a stimulus but, after it had been rejected, the happy thought occurred to me that if I could hear what had stimulated his music at times when his muse had spoken to him, I might be able to provide that stimulus myself."

I must have looked a little blank.

"That Prelude we heard, good Watson, opens as a tolling bell and I have subsequently researched it and found it echoes the bell of the Kremlin in Russia's old capital city, Moscow. One publisher has even issued a version of it under the title *Bells of Moscow*. To take Rachmaninov to hear a toll of bells after we had heard a piece of his own featuring the tolling of a bell, seemed to me to be a stratagem worth trying. It seemed especially appropriate to take him to a bell toll which has been set to the words 'I do not know' although I was not to know how he would handle it in his own music."

"But why did he not see that it was you that had prompted that rather than me?"

"So, dear Watson, you are now wise enough to see my *modus operandi?*" asked Holmes slyly.

I confined myself to a slightly rueful smile and Holmes continued.

"I fear, good Watson, that here you are venturing into a world where I have perhaps got to the limits of where my methods can be applied. One might attribute the composer's reaction to his excitement at being able to write again, but the common theme of what we have observed throughout these matters is that in Russia everything is different from here in England for all that there are superficial similarities as well."

Holmes paused and puffed his pipe before he continued.

"These differences are not confined to minor things. The calendar including the date of Christmas, the alphabet, the naming conventions, the railway gauges, the form of greeting, the cigarettes, the bestowal of justice, the role of the monarch, the music criticism, the attitude to alcohol – all are different. We are fortunate in this country that we do not have to live subject to whims of an autarch for you saw the consequences of that for poor Ivanov. The Russians seem to have had nothing but an autarch as their leader, and I will be surprised if any successor of the present Tsar is different."

Another pause and another puff.

"That there are aspects of Rachmaninov's behaviour we do not understand – his preference to consulting with you rather than with me, the attribution of his consultation's success to you rather than to me, how he chose to translate the tolling of the Bow bells into his new concerto – should perhaps also not surprise us. The Russian psyche remains to the English observer truly – what did my brother say? – a riddle wrapped in a mystery inside an enigma."

Note by Henry Durham, historical advisor to
The Redacted Sherlock Holmes

This work picks up from *The Golden Pince-Nez*. The picture on the left is of that work's final scene. From left to right, are Anna, Stanley Hopkins, Sherlock Holmes, Dr Watson, and Professor Coram.

The scenes of Holmes and Watson, Count Baron Egor Egorovich Staal, Mikhael Artemyevich Muravyov, and Czar Nicholaus II bear a striking similarity to Kafka's short story *Before the Law* which Kafka also inserted into his novel *The Trial*. Readers of other books in *The Redacted Sherlock Holmes* series will know from *Volume IV* that Holmes and Watson met Franz Kafka and Franz Kafka's father, Hermann, on 19 November 1910 – thus before Kafka had written *Before the Law* in either version.

Dr Watson's influence on Kafka's writing is a fertile field for literary analysis as *Volume III* of the *Redacted* series contains the work on which Kafka based his masterpiece, *The Trial*, and it is hard to imagine how Kafka might have written it if he had not been in direct correspondence with Dr Watson.

The Queen, the Dame, and the Left-Footer

I have commented elsewhere that 1895 was a year of quite unsurpassed professional success for my friend. This did not apply to the petition he received from illustrious writer, Mr Oscar Wilde, who had been arraigned for acts that I cannot describe in any detail here, but which will, I am sure, be known to my readers whenever this work may be read. The poet had asked Holmes's help to counter the charges, but my friend's investigations only confirmed the accuracy of their substance, and in the end Holmes withdrew from the commission – an event which happened more often than anyone might think who has known my friend only from the works published in my lifetime.

By the time the case ended – having attracted the most prurient interest from the whole of the press – Holmes had distanced himself from it entirely and expressed relief to me that he had done so. On the day the verdict was announced, he and I had gone for a walk in Regent's Park.

"A new case," said Holmes, his face brightening at the sight of a waiting hansom at our door as we returned, "and our client must be a man of substance to pay for a cab to wait until I return."

Sitting at the fireside of our quarters was the massively built Mycroft Holmes, whom, to avoid confusion, I shall continue to call Mycroft, while I refer to his brother, Sherlock, as Holmes.

If my readers ever have the chance to read those works of mine that I have seen fit to redact from the published canon, they will have noted how often Mycroft appears. Sometimes he came to Baker Street, at other times he issued a summons for Holmes and me to come to the Diogenes Club. Almost all our interactions with him related to great matters of state which, as my reader will understand, could not be disclosed to the public in my lifetime. That Mycroft now wanted to talk to Holmes and me about a matter of state this did not surprise me but, as my reader will discover, what followed took in several quite unprecedented twists and matters did not come to what I can only regard as a somewhat inconclusive end until several decades had elapsed.

"Matters in Patagonia," began Mycroft with no word of greeting, "are coming to a head. And, yet here I am, compelled to leave my office to deal with a 'love that dares not speak its name'. It really is most inconvenient."

"Perhaps, brother Mycroft," said Holmes, with the ease of a man without any weighty matter on his mind, "you might like to be more precise about the reason why you are here."

"The matter arises out of the legalities of the Wilde case just past."

"I would have thought," replied Holmes drily, "that whatever one's view of the decision to bring a prosecution, the facts of the case were clear. And the legalities of it have been similarly plain since the passing of the Labouchere amendment in Section 11 of the Criminal Law Amendment Act of ten years ago. The amendment made illegal any intimacy between men, even if it involves no physical contact."

I think Mycroft was surprised at my colleague's swift and informed response and Holmes gestured at me before saying, "My biographer here has referred to me as having a good practical knowledge of English Law."

"What you say, Sherlock, is of course true. But the legislation as it stands applies only to men. Since the conclusion of the trial, the Prime Minister has been most insistent that we look to have similar and specific legislation introduced for women. Lord Rosebury has commented that we live in times where women are being given similar rights as men and with similar rights come similar obligations."

"Was this not looked at in 1885?"

"Indeed it was, dear Sherlock, but there was a problem."

Mycroft sat in silence. An unwonted looked of puzzlement came across my friend's face while he waited for Mycroft to continue but there was a long pause before Mycroft spoke again.

"I have, good brother," he came up with at last, "perhaps in my agitation at being unable to pursue our interests in Patagonia to this country's best advantage, already said more to you than I should have done about this." He rose as if to leave. "It was in fact not you but your colleague Dr Watson here, whom I came here to consult. Doctor, you will have seen a hansom cab waiting for us on the street below. Could I ask you to join me?"

My readers may wonder why I followed Mycroft Holmes's request to come with him without asking any questions but there was a masterfulness about Mycroft's manner which made it very hard not to do what he said. I have never seen my friend look so crestfallen as when, in the company of Mycroft, I rose and passed through the door of our sitting-room, down the seventeen stairs, and out to the cab below.

"The problem we have had with banning the sort of behaviour Mr Wilde has engaged in between women," explained Mycroft when we were seated, "is that Her Majesty, Queen Victoria, declined to believe that any woman would want engage in...ahem… any such activity with another woman. She refused to sign the 1885 act into law unless it referred only to males."

"So how can I help?"

"You are the best-known doctor in the land and, having been married and with your experience of medical practice, you have a much wider experience of women than either I or, I suspect, my brother. You thus offer a blend of plausibility and experience quite beyond what my brother and I have to offer."

"So what do you want me to say?"

"I was really hoping that you would be able to come up with that, dear Doctor. My brother has always commented negatively about your fecund imagination. Now is the time to use that fecund imagination to positive advantage."

Mycroft Holmes was not a man given to small talk and we sat in silence as the cab rattled down Regent Street and into the Mall before drawing up outside Buckingham Palace.

All the while we went, I gave consideration of what I arguments I might make. It was not long before we were brought into an elaborate state room and were joined by the black-clad and aged monarch.

"Really, Mr Holmes," said she to Mycroft in a querulous voice when he put the matter to her, "this is something we discussed when this Act of Parliament was originally passed a decade or so ago and I do not think that anything has changed since."

She paused before continuing.

"I am still in mourning for dear Albert," she went on before pausing and had to dab her eye with a black fringed lace handkerchief at the recollection of her late husband. "I must say that it is most troubling that you should have seen fit to raise this matter all over again, Mr Holmes."

"The Prime Minister was most insistent, Ma'am, that I raise the matter with you."

"When I think back long ago to the embrace of my dear Albert, Mr Holmes," replied the Queen to Mycroft – and for the first time there was a softening of her features at what was clearly a cherished memory – "the idea that a woman would seek comfort…. in the arms of another woman is utterly inconceivable. When I first lay in Albert's arms, Mr Holmes, I could not believe that people who were not of royal blood were allowed similar pleasures. You, Mr Holmes, and your brother, whom I see almost as often as I see you as he receives state honours for his criminal work, are unattached and are men. I fear that you and he would not understand."

A far-away look came into her eye.

"When I think of the embrace of Albert…" she said, referencing her late husband yet again. A shudder seemed to course through her body as her voice, which had acquired a tinge of sweetness as she recalled her late husband, trailed off into silence.

"Indeed so, Ma'am," interjected Mycroft, looking a little unsure of himself. "It is for that reason that I have brought along Dr Watson, who has a wider experience of the generality of life than either I or my brother, so that he can explain matters in such a way that you may give them fresh consideration."

"Very well, Dr Watson," said the Queen, in a voice laden with scepticism and suspicion, "what have you to say?"

"Ma'am," I said, "legislation of this kind is designed to give legal protection to those who do not wish to engage in activities,"…I looked for a way of avoiding the repetition of "of this kind," but my vaunted imagination failed me and in the end I was obliged rather lamely to repeat it.

"Dr Watson," said the Queen, her voice acquiring a new briskness, "perhaps you should set out your qualifications for speaking to me on this matter."

I had not expected this response, and it took a little time before I came out with, "I have served as an army doctor and have had general medical practices in Paddington and Kensington. I have also obtained a wide view of life in my collaborations with Mr Sherlock Holmes."

"And in all the wide view of life you have described, have you ever encountered two women engaging in the sorts of things we are discussing among anyone you know."

In the army I had dealt only with men. In civil practice no woman had spoken to me of such matters. I struggled to find a response to the Queen's question, the silence in the room became overwhelming. In the end the best I could come out with was, "Ma'am, I have heard tell of it," which was true but did not really answer the question.

The queen saw through my evasiveness and rejoindered, "And I have heard tell of Father Christmas."

"If such behaviour were to become widespread, there would be fewer people for your nation and fewer servicemen for the armed forces," was the best I could come up with as a response.

"Dr Watson," came the reply in a voice I can only describe as haughty, "you are here to represent a wider view of life than that offered by Mr Mycroft Holmes and yet you have never encountered a case of this kind. Thus, very clearly it is not in any way widespread, and your response is theoretical at best. And at its worst, it is inventing a problem that does not exist."

I was at a loss for words and the Queen now turned to Mycroft.

"Your specialism, Mr Holmes, has been described by your brother as omniscience. This means all-knowing. Have you, Mr Mycroft Holmes, in your all-knowing state ever suspected any women of partaking in such activities?"

"Indeed not, Ma'am. My work is for the country and its Empire," replied Mycroft, perhaps a little loftily. "It is with politicians who are male who are voted for by a male electorate, and with civil servants who are also male."

"Quite so," replied the Queen briskly, and another long silence followed before the Queen asked Mycroft, "Mr Holmes, is the governance of my country and its empire so straightforward, that it has no real as opposed to theoretical problems to solve?"

Mycroft had no response to this.

"And is my sex given the same rights in property and in voting so that it should also have the same restrictions on its behaviour imposed on it?"

I think Mycroft realised that he and I had done all that we could, and he beat a tactical withdrawal.

"Maybe, good doctor," he mused a little forlornly, as we sat once more in a hansom, "I am not so omniscient as my brother has described me."

Mycroft's quarters were only a few short yards from Buckingham Palace, and he soon descended while I returned to Baker Street with the stern injunction to say nothing of what had occurred to my fellow tenant, Sherlock Holmes. When I crossed the threshold of our sitting-room it was to find my friend sitting with a client – a tall, tweed-clad woman of about thirty-five. There was an elaborate tricorn hat on an occasional table beside her. She was speaking as I entered and the first words I heard her say were:

"I wonder often why it is so much easier for me – as I believe it is for a great many English women – to love my own sex passionately than to love yours, Mr Holmes. I can't make it out, for I am a very healthy-minded person."

"Take a seat, good Watson," cried Holmes when he saw me. "My client is Miss Ethel Smyth, who has a matter to discuss that is to my knowledge unique and also highly personal. Perhaps, Miss Smyth, you might like to tell Dr Watson and me a little more about yourself before we move onto the subject of your petition."

"My name, as you say, Mr Holmes, is Ethel Smyth. I am making my way through life as a musician."

"That is most remarkable. As a pianist, I take it, Miss Smyth. Your spatulate finger ends would imply as much although your ruddy complexion also implies much time spent in the fresh air."

"I am an excellent pianist, Mr Holmes, but it is as a composer I would wish to make my name. My father was utterly against the idea. But I eventually persuaded him to allow me to study composition in Leipzig in Germany."

"How did you do that?"

"Oh, I sat in my room and starved myself until he changed his mind. I went without food for nearly two weeks. Eventually he caved in," said Miss Smyth with the breezy air of someone who regarded hunger-striking as the merest bagatelle.

"Pray continue."

"When I got to Leipzig, I started at the Conservatoire, but I was disappointed with the teaching there and ended up taking private lessons with a gentleman called Heinrich von Herzogenberg. His wife was called Elisabeth. She and I became," – Miss Smyth broke off as she considered a suitable formulation for what she wanted to say – "passionate about each other – I will not disclose any more – and remained so for as long as I was in Leipzig."

I suppose the sentence I had heard from Miss Smyth when I entered the sitting-room ought to have meant that the last sentence of the last paragraph should not have startled me as much as it did, but I must here state that, perhaps influenced by my previous interview with Queen Victoria, that I would be surprised if a look of shock did not come across my face.

Holmes for his part looked entirely unperturbed.

"I see," said he. "And what has happened to Frau von Herzogenberg?"

"Dearest Lisl had a weak heart and died two years ago in a health resort on the Italian Riviera where she had gone as a rest-cure in the company of her husband. But I have had a string of other women as lovers since then."

"Have you had any male lovers?"

"There was and is Henry Bennet Brewster who has written the libretto for an opera I have composed. He is married to Lisl's sister."

I think Holmes was about to say something, but Miss Smyth added, "I have been…." she paused as she again sought the right words but in the end confined herself to repeating the ambiguous formulation… "passionate about his wife as well. And she about me."

"And why do you wish to see me?"

"I confess Mr Holmes, it was actually both you and Dr Watson I wished to consult. You are one of the minds of the age, Mr Holmes, and Dr Watson is the best-known doctor in the land. There is no legal limitation on my amatory activities at present, but after the verdict in the trial of Mr Oscar Wilde yesterday, I am concerned that it may not be long in coming. I wanted advice from Dr Watson on whether I am suffering from a medical condition and from you if there is anything you recommend I should do."

Holmes paused and reached into his pocket for his pipe.

"I take it, madame, you have no objection to tobacco?" he enquired.

"I feared you would never ask, Mr Holmes," replied our visitor breezily and, while Holmes lit his pipe and I lit a cigarette, Miss Smyth reached into her pocket and took out a fat cigar and a device which I had never seen before. There was a sharp snipping sound, as Miss Smyth made practised use of a cigar-cutter. With a satisfied sigh, she leant back in the chair, and issued a sigh of contentment as she took her first puff of her cigar. The tip glowed vermillion, and a column of aromatic and silvery smoke rose into the air.

In the end it was Holmes who spoke, and he addressed his words to me.

"Do you consider that this falls into your ambit, good doctor?"

As my reader will already know, although Holmes did not, I had never done more than hear of a case such as this. I wondered whether I should disclose this but, in the end, I confined myself to saying, "My treatments for complaints of all sorts are mainly the administration of brandy and a recommendation to increase the amount one smokes. I do not think either of these treatments will be of use in a case such as this."

Holmes was about to speak again before Miss Smyth interjected.

"I do not consider myself in anything other than in rude physical health, gentlemen. I play tennis, I am an indefatigable golfer, and I ride most days, which is why I have the ruddy complexion that Mr Holmes has observed."

She paused and puffed her cigar as though not sure what she should say next.

"I must confess, Mr Holmes," she said continuing as last, "to a slight sense of disappointment that you made an inference about me no more precise than that I spend a lot of time in the fresh air rather than being specific about what I do when I am there. I would have thought my bowed gait should have betrayed my love of the ride." She paused and her gaze fixed first on Holmes and then on me and back. "When I am not following my outdoor pursuits, I am either writing music or trying to arrange performances for my music. I also write ardently about music."

"Dear madame," said Holmes, "the course of life you have chosen to follow is very much your own. And you have found many things to engage your time. You seem to be living life to the full at present."

"Is that all you have to say, Mr Holmes?"

"It seems to me that there is no law that can touch you," continued Holmes, "although I cannot, of-course, rule out such a law being introduced in the future. And the matters which you fear might become subject to it, seem all to have taken place outside this country."

I think Miss Smyth was about to interrupt at this point, for she opened her mouth as if to do so but in the end she let my friend's comment pass, and Holmes continued.

"I may say that some of my followers have raised questions of a personal nature about me. That was why I disbanded the Baker Street Irregulars as soon as I became well known through the writings of my biographer here as I wished to avoid any association with street-boys. I am now engaged in investigation after investigation up and down the land and, when I have no such investigation on hand, I produce monographs on subjects as diverse as tattoos and tobacco ash. I also play the violin and conduct experiments in chemistry. When the beloved wife of the good doctor here passed from this life, I recommended that he use his work as a distraction. If it is a distraction you are seeking then I can only recommend that you do as many different things as you can."

"I was quite taken up by religion a few years ago and wrote a setting of the Mass which was nearly an hour in length.

But I fear my passion for religion has passed," said Miss Smyth thoughtfully. "Maybe I should look for something else to engage my energies."

Holmes had no response to this.

Miss Smyth followed up with further questions, but the substance of what Holmes said did not change, and in the end she withdrew. My readers may understand that I was in something of a quandary as to what to say to Holmes given the interview I had had with Queen Victoria to which I had been sworn to secrecy by Mycroft. Equally, I was unsure whether I should draw Miss Smyth's petition to the attention of Mycroft, especially as there had been no specific instruction to keep what Miss Smyth had said to Holmes and me confidential. After much reflection, I felt obliged to tell Mycroft what had happened to see if he wanted to revert to Queen Victoria with the information that we had identified a woman with a desire for other women. I did so without disclosing Miss Smyth's identity.

Mycroft was not normally a man given to self-doubt and was, I suspect, still nursing his wounds from our encounter with the monarch. All he said was, "So you have told me about a woman to whom you have given the name Smith, and you say she plays the piano? Given what Her Majesty had to say, I doubt that one woman called Smith – much the commonest name in the country – and who plays the piano – which is the preferred pastime of most under-occupied woman – moves the needle. Unlike Mr Wilde, whatever the woman whose activities you have brought to my attention chooses to do, she will not attract interest across the land."

He paused and took a pinch of snuff before concluding, "It would be otiose indeed to subject ourselves to another interview with Her Majesty on this topic so I think we should let the matter rest. That will also have the happy result that I can dedicate myself once more to Patagonia."

For my part I followed the activities of Miss Smyth closely, which, contrary to what Mycroft had said, proved easy to do.

I was impressed when towards the end of '90s Miss Smyth sent Holmes the score of a string quartet, but I confess to having been filled with a sense of awe when Miss Smyth's opera *Der Wald* or *The Forest*, became the first opera by a woman to be staged at the Metropolitan Opera in New York (*Editorial note*: the next time an opera composed by a woman was staged at the Metropolitan Opera was in 2016, more than one hundred years later).

If my readers, at some future juncture, are impressed by these feats, they may be astonished to find out about the next time she came to my attention.

In 1912 an account appeared in *The Times* of how she had thrown stones through the windows of the private home of Colonial Secretary, Mr Lewis Harcourt. Miss Smyth had become an ardent campaigner for votes for women or suffragism and had been motivated to attack Mr Harcourt's home by his comment that if all women were as well-behaved and intelligent as his wife, they would have got the vote long ago. The newspaper described how she shouted "Six!" as each stone struck home. She was sentenced to two months in the women's prison at Holloway for her offence where she joined numerous other women who had been convicted of other offences in the same cause.

While in custody, Miss Smyth was to spend much of her time on hunger-strike. My practice was close to Holloway Prison, and I was asked to visit her and fellow hunger-strikers to assess their condition.

As I passed through the forbidding entrance of the prison, I could hear singing from the yard and, when I entered the yard, I saw women parading in a square and singing a chorus which began with the words "March! March!" I assume the music had been composed by Miss Smyth, for I could see her at the window of her cell vigorously directing the singing below with a toothbrush in her hand.

"I have not eaten food for six days," she said briskly to me, when I saw her, "but I find that my energy is unabated." My subsequent examination of her only confirmed her own assessment.

Holmes had long left London for what I thought was his retirement and, when I drew Miss Smyth's conduct to his attention on one of his very infrequent visits to London, he commented, "Campaigning for votes for women has certainly given her something to engage her energies, and I am glad she has avoided scandal about anything else."

Hard on the heels of this came the outbreak of the First World War.

Suddenly there were no men to do the work they had traditionally done, and women took over everything from factory-working to bus-driving. All places of entertainment – theatres, the new picture houses, sports grounds – were closed. By the end of the war, the world had been transformed and, amongst the transformations it wrought, was the granting of votes to women who were able to vote for the first time in the general election held in December 1918, a month after the signing of the Armistice.

It was in February 1921 that a somewhat harassed-looking Mycroft Holmes stood on my doorstep in Queen Anne Street early one morning and asked to be admitted in a tone that brooked no argument. I had no sooner let him in when an oddly sheepish looking Sherlock Holmes arrived carrying an overnight bag.

"We may now be living in a land fit for heroes to live in," started Mycroft, "but some things do not change."

If Mycroft had been a client, Holmes would have used the charm he always had at his disposal though seldom felt any need to deploy, to elicit a more detailed petition. As it was, he said, "I take it from the telegram you sent demanding my attendance here, that it is the issue of women and…" Holmes paused as, uncharacteristically, he had to look for the right word, "…women that you wish to raise, and contrary to our discussions of 1895, you wish this time to involve me fully in the discussions."

"In 1895 it was Lord Rosebury. Now it is David Lloyd George. Prime ministers come and prime ministers go but their petty concerns remain the same. The Patagonia issue of a quarter of a century ago is still not resolved to this nation's best advantage and the Prime Minister has summoned me back from retirement to look once more at the 'love which dares not say its name.'"

Mycroft paused, and as was his wont when deeply moved, took a large pinch of snuff.

"Women's Association Football," he came out with at last to my considerable surprise.

In the works I have allowed to be published in my lifetime, I have covered horse-racing and rugby but never what I regarded as the working man's game.

"Women's teams are playing Association Football, or soccer as it is sometimes called. Women's football started as a way to boost morale when women began working in factories during the war just ended, and it has taken off both as an activity for women and as a spectator sport. The women attract huge crowds among what I can only describe as the meaner class of people," added Mycroft, a note of disgruntlement in his voice.

"Are the women professional?"

"They play to raise money for the millions of servicemen and their families who have fallen on hard times following deaths or wounds at the front. The main recipient of the money they raise is the National Association of Discharged and Disabled Soldiers and Sailors."

I could not, in the egalitarian world we now found ourselves living in, understand what the objection could be to this, although the concept of women playing a team sport involving physical contact was new to me.

"The best-known player," continued Mycroft, "is called Miss Lily Parr. She started as a munitions worker or munitionette, as they were known when they worked."

Mycroft paused to take more snuff and there was another long pause.

"*The Tatler*, a gossip magazine of the lowest sort and serially unreliable as a source of information, is about to reveal that she..." Mycroft paused once more as he sought a suitable expression... "enjoys the embrace of one of her fellow women-footballers."

Another pinch of snuff and then Mycroft continued.

"Were Miss Parr to be someone not known to the masses, this behaviour would not be of interest to anyone. As it is, the games she is involved in and in which she is the best player, draw crowds in their thousands. If the association she has with her team-mate were to become widely known, it might encourage other women to…well, to do the same thing…especially as the people who attend these women's games come from a social class that is impressionable in a way that better educated people are not."

Mycroft paused again before delivering himself of his next remark.

"It is the way with the sexes. To stop a man doing something, you place an explicit ban on it. To stop a woman doing something, you merely make sure her attention is not drawn to it. It is as Eve in the Garden of Eden. She had ignored the apples on the tree until her attention was drawn to them by the serpent. We all know what happened once the serpent had done his work, and I can think of no better way of drawing women's interest to the matters we have been discussing than an article in *The Tatler* about a woman whose activity is keenly followed by the masses. Who knows how matters may end after that? And what will happen in Patagonia while my focus is away from it?"

"What is it you want me to do, Mycroft?" cut in Holmes. "You have surely not brought me to London from Sussex merely to complain about not being able to focus your energies on Patagonia."

"Indeed not, Sherlock. I want you to go and investigate whether the story that *The Tatler* is due to run is true. If it is false, we can easily explode it. If, on the other hand, it is true, I will have to undertake other measures to ensure that it does not attract attention. I would wish that Dr Watson goes with you and makes a record of what you discover as his word will be believed before all others."

"You want me to investigate something that is not now and never has been in any sense illegal and that may or may not be taking place in private between two adults who both consent to it?" asked Holmes.

"It is you who express it in that way."

"I express it in that way because it states matters as they stand," said Holmes robustly.

"Only you, dear Sherlock, have the necessary finesse to carry out such investigations given your experience in the petty matters of the police court," said Mycroft, a quite unwonted tone of wheedling coming into his voice. "This is not a police matter as no crime is being committed under the present legislation. And, of course, there is no other investigator – and no other chronicler of the investigation," here Mycroft nodded at me – "whom I would trust on a matter of such sensitivity."

I was not at all sure whether Holmes was going to accept the commission, but, in the end, he agreed. He spent the rest of the morning surrounded by newspapers, went out at lunchtime, and came back with several bags over his shoulder.

"We are off," he said to me at breakfast the next day. "As Mycroft said, Miss Parr's team started in a munitions factory. It was called Dick, Kerr Limited, and so the football team had the name Dick, Kerr Ladies. It is due to play against a team representative of the rest of Britain at two o'clock this afternoon. Please bring with you a bag for an overnight stay."

I had my practice to attend to but, such was the joy of working with Holmes again, I made sure I was able to pass the work on to others. Soon we were at Euston, and soon after that we were flying north-west in first-class.

When I took a look at my friend, it struck me that I had never seen him as unsure of himself as he appeared to be now. The unsure expression remained on his face as we headed from Liverpool Lime Street towards Anfield Football Stadium. "I see myself as the protagonist in the battle between right and wrong," he said to me at one point. "Here I am not at all sure I represent right, and I do not see that we are investigating something that is wrong."

At least we had no difficulty finding the way as even half a mile from the ground everybody we saw was heading in one direction and, as Mycroft had foreshadowed, we were soon in a crowd of thousands. Holmes bought a programme which I noted he studied closely once we had taken seats. As soon as the game started, it was obvious which was the stronger side and who was the best player in that stronger side.

Holmes was utterly beguiled by the spectacle and the speeches that follow were said by him in a breathless tone that I can only describe as star-struck, "Miss Parr is truly an Amazon!"….. "Six-foot tall, raven hair, and swift as a gazelle!"… "She kicks the ball with the ferocity of a mule and the precision of a surgeon"…"She is so like me – tall, athletic, and a straight left – she with her boot on the football-field and me with my fist in the boxing-ring."

So enraptured was he that it was a complete surprise when, with twenty minutes of the game left to go with Dick, Kerr Ladies seven goals to one up over the Rest of Britain and with Miss Parr having scored four goals, Holmes rose and said, "Come, Watson, we have work to do."

I followed him from our seat and out of the ground. He walked around the outside of the stadium until he found a bus and its driver.

"Good sir," he said, in a voice with a sudden and unexpected Liverpool accent but with a quavering tone that made him sound much older than he was, "can you tell me which bus to take to the station? I want to get there before the crowd comes out and bowls me over. I am not as young as I was."

"God bless you, sir. Also a supporter of the Dick, Kerr Ladies? And having to leave early? Station's a while away. I'd drive you and your friend there if I could, but I need to be ready for the ladies when they come out."

"I would have thought that the players would make their own way home."

"Oh no, they're playing in London tomorrow, so they're staying in Liverpool tonight, and going there by train in the morning."

"And aren't the young ladies going to their hotel on foot?"

"They'd be recognised on the street, and they'd never get there. Even when they're inside a hotel, their food has to be brought to their rooms. They are so well-known now that they would never be left alone in a public area. Anyway, I am afraid I can't spend all day talking," he said as a long peep from a whistle from inside the stadium told us that the game was over. "They'll be out soon, and I have to be ready for them. Take the road opposite that gate there." He pointed. "The number 74 goes straight to Lime Street."

"Well, that was easy enough," said Holmes, sounding like his normal self, as we went through the gate to which the driver had pointed. "I had a fifty per cent chance of picking the right bus and a fifty per cent chance that the ladies were staying in Liverpool rather than getting the train down tonight, and overnighting in London. And there will be very few hotels in Liverpool that offer their guests room service."

Rather than taking the bus, Holmes hailed a cab. Once in the seats for passengers, he got two jackets of the sort worn by commissionaires out of his overnight bag. He handed one to me, and put his own jacket and mine into the bag in their place. Back in the centre of Liverpool, Holmes went to the main flower shop in the centre and bought the largest bouquet of flowers I have ever seen. We then went to the Railway Hotel and Holmes asked to leave the bouquet for a Miss Parr on behalf of an admirer. He was be told that there was no such guest staying but unabashed we went first to the Mersey Hotel, where we got the same response, and then to the six storey Grand Hotel where the receptionist said, "Ah yes, of course".

He called an attendant over and said to him, "Another bouquet for Room 612. This time it's for Miss Lily Parr rather than for Miss Alice Wood."

Holmes and I were soon back on the street and Holmes rubbed his hands together with glee. "The years pass, good Watson, but I trust that age has not withered my ability to bring light to which is obscure to others. We will be back tonight."

Holmes found a hotel for us, his good humour continuing and his look of uncertainty a memory of the morning.

"We will return to the Grand at seven," he said.

A quarter to seven saw us depart, this time dressed in outfits common to waiting staff, and we entered the hotel from the rear.

"Now we go to the kitchen," said my friend, "and wait for an order for room 612."

We had not long to wait as next time the chef set down trays it was with the cry of "For room 612!"

We went up in the lift and left the trays outside the door.

"Let us hide in the stairwell," said Holmes. "We are on the sixth floor in a building with a lift. No one will use the stairs."

The Red-Headed League, *The Hound of the Baskervilles*, *The Speckled Band* – they all required long waits in pitch darkness. But the wait in the dimly lit and bare stairwell as we investigated a matter of greater prurience that I had ever looked at with my friend had a character of its own.

"The trays are out," said Holmes at a quarter past nine but Holmes waited until a quarter to ten before we ventured out to collect them. When we did so, there emanated from room 612, sounds which, though faint, could indicate only one thing.

"Come Watson," whispered Holmes to me after a few seconds, a disturbed look on his face, "I think we have heard enough." A few minutes later and we were back at our hotel.

Homes said nothing to me that night or the next morning as we took the train back to London. On his face he wore the same serious and concerned look as he had done the previous morning as we had headed up to Liverpool, and he filled and refilled his pipe almost obsessively throughout the journey. It was only as we were pulling into Euston Station that he said to me, "I do not know what I would do should I have had the good fortune to be the father of so singular a daughter as Miss Parr. But my previous remarks that she has done nothing illegal and nothing to which the other party has not consented still apply. I would beg you to say nothing of what we have discovered to Mycroft."

When we got to Queen Square, it was to find Mycroft already there.

"I reasoned," he said, "that you would go to Liverpool on the train and hence I expected you back today. What are your findings, dear brother?"

"I saw nothing untoward, Mycroft. My only observation is that Miss Parr is a remarkable woman in every way."

"But that is no answer! Did your investigation not uncover any evidence of the matters we discussed?"

"I would refer you to my previous response on this matter. I saw nothing untoward."

"What is your comment, doctor?" asked Mycroft turning to me.

"In matters of investigation, I would always defer to your brother."

Mycroft turned back to Holmes.

"So, you and your colleague would defy me?"

"I am someone whom you consult, dear Mycroft. I am not someone to whom you give instructions."

"Very well, good brother," said Mycroft smoothly. "You have obviously become a conscientious objector." He turned to me. "I wonder if you might come with me, Dr Watson. When one is dealing with high matters of state, it is always good to have a chronicler whom others will believe even if I believe you are being less than straightforward with me on this matter."

As though in a daze, I followed Mycroft to the door and, as he went through it, Mycroft turned to Holmes and said, "I am sure you will be able to make your own way out of the doctor's house, dear brother."

It was only when we were on the street that I thought to ask Mycroft where we were going.

"To Lancaster Gate," said he, and we were soon climbing the steps to the headquarters of football's governing body, the Football Association, where Mycroft's visiting card immediately obtained for us an interview with the organization's president, Lord Kinnaird.

He was a giant of a man and, although in his seventies with a long grey beard, he looked as though he were ready once more to bestride the sporting fields as he had when he had played nine times in the so-called FA Cup Final, a knock-out tournament run under the auspices of the Football Association.

"The government is," began Mycroft without preamble, "very concerned about the spread of football among women."

"To me," replied Kinnaird in a considered tone, "it is a sport most unfitting for women. When I played, I always played so that if I came home with a broken leg, it was unlikely to be my own. I do not think that such a comment is likely to be made of some gentle maiden who takes up the game."

"Indeed so. If women engage in pastimes such as football, they are unlikely to put their energies into matters that are of value to the nation such as child-bearing and child-rearing. This is a matter of particular concern after a war which has greatly reduced the number of men available for service. The Prime Minister is most concerned about it as one cannot be sure when the next war will be."

"I understand your concerns, Mr Holmes," said Kinnaird, "and share them. And I also have the fear that popular interest in the women's game will draw crowds and hence money away from the game played by men. But I cannot ban women from playing football."

"You may not be able to stop them playing, my Lord," replied Mycroft quietly, "but you can stop them drawing large crowds."

"How so?" asked Kinnaird, looking surprised but engaged.

"You could withdraw membership of the Football Association from the clubs who allow women who use their facilities. That would mean those clubs that allow use of such facilities will not be able to take part in any of your competitions. They will thus be impelled to prohibit women from playing on their grounds while the men's game will continue as it is. If large crowds of people can no longer watch football played by women but can continue to watch football played by men, interest in football played by women will soon dwindle."

"What you say is true," said Kinnaird to Mycroft thoughtfully.

"I suggest that the Football Association issues a statement saying something like this, 'Complaints having been made as to football being played by women. The Council of the Football Association feels impelled to express its strong opinion that the game of football is quite unsuitable for females and ought not to be encouraged. Accordingly, the Council instructs the clubs belonging to the Association to refuse the use of their grounds for matches played by women.' I think that will cover it."

The statement was in the press the following day, much to the distress of the organizers of football matches for women. In the end Miss Parr's team was forced to play their matches abroad and interest in them in Britain soon abated although, on the rare occasions Holmes and I met in the years that followed, I noted he was as abreast of Miss Parr's team and of her performances for it as a proud father might be. And although her following was greatly diminished among the general public, no newspaper or other organ ever thought it worthwhile to produce a prurient article about Miss Parr.

By contrast, in spite of being a convicted felon, albeit to effect a change in the law that had subsequently been enacted, Miss Smyth's music-making gave her such a following among this country's intellectual elite, who were, in Mycroft's opinion, not as impressionable as the masses, that she was made Dame Ethel Smyth in 1924.

Note by Henry Durham, historical advisor to
The Redacted Sherlock Holmes

For someone accused by no less a figure than Sherlock Holmes of romanticising events, Dr Watson's account above is accurate in terms of both dates and historical detail. Miss Parr is in the bottom left-hand corner of the cover and her preference for the left foot - her shot was said to be the hardest from any man or woman in England – is obvious. Ethel Smyth or Dame Ethel Smyth, as she became, is next to her.

The bar on women-players using the facilities of the top Association Football Clubs imposed by the Football Association when Lord Kinnaird (pictured left) was president was not lifted until 1971 when the Women's Football Association was founded.

The Bohemian Corporal

And yet even to the powers of my friend, Mr Sherlock Holmes, and to those of his even abler brother, Mycroft, there are limits. The matter I relate below gives an example of where they both failed, although here they failed where no one else succeeded. Indeed, no one else got anywhere like as far as they, and, above all, Mycroft got. That does not of course mitigate the consequences of this failure.

In the years after the end of the Great War, I continued to run my medical practice in Queen Anne Street. The history books will record that London at this time was full of demobilised soldiers many of whom still showing the after-effects of wounds and gassing, and of civilians suffering from Spanish flu and its aftermath. With the normal onerous workload of a medical practice, I was thus never at less than full stretch. In the end I was obliged to employ two other doctors in my practice to take the strain.

At this point of my life, my contact with my friend Mr Sherlock Holmes had been no more than infrequent for several years although, as I have commented elsewhere, he did use my home for London meetings as his retirement to Sussex meant he no longer had a place for meeting clients in the capital. As the notice I got of such meetings was often the briefest, I came to regard such impositions as the price of our continued friendship.

It was late on the evening of Sunday the 15th of February 1920 that there was a knock on the door and, as it was past the servants' waking hours, I answered it myself fearing a medical emergency and an all-night patient visit. On the step stood Sherlock Holmes carrying a large case.

"My dear fellow," said I, "pray come in."

"You look surprised, and no wonder! Relieved that you are not being called out too, I fancy! Hum! I see, even thirty years on, you still smoke the Arcadia mixture of your bachelor days! There's no mistaking that fluffy ash upon your lapel. It is good that the easing of the restraints of supply now that the war is over means that it is available once more. And it's easy to tell that you have been accustomed to wear a uniform, Watson. You'll never pass as a pure-bred civilian as long as you keep that habit of carrying your handkerchief in your sleeve. Could you put me up tonight?"

"With pleasure," I replied.

"You told me that you had bachelor quarters for one, and I see that you have no gentleman visitor at present. Your hat-stand proclaims as much."

"I shall be delighted if you will stay."

"Thank you. I'll fill the vacant peg then. Sorry to see that you've had the British workman in the house. He's a token of evil. Not the drains, I hope?"

"No, the gas."

"Ah! He has left two nail-marks from his boot upon your linoleum just where the light strikes it. No, thank you, I had some supper at Victoria, but I'll smoke a pipe with you with pleasure."

I handed him my pouch, and he seated himself opposite to me.

He took a pinch of tobacco from the pouch, rubbed it meditatively between the tips of his long, thin fingers, filled his pipe, struck a match, and then sat in contentment as the mellow smoke rose from the bowl. A thoughtful look came over his face as he smoked for some time in silence. I was well aware that only business of importance would have brought him to me at such an hour, and so I waited patiently until he should come round to it.

"Would you, good Watson, still rate my knowledge and understanding of politics as feeble?" he asked at length.

"That was a judgment I made over forty years ago," I replied cautiously, recalling the list of my friend's limitations which I had compiled soon after I had first met him.

"Visiting us tomorrow is a man from Munich," replied my friend in what sounded like a *non sequitur*.

"Visiting us?" I exclaimed. While I was delighted to see Holmes, I was by no means sure I wanted a second person, and a stranger at that, under my roof especially as the size of Holmes's bag suggested a stay longer than one night. At this point, as I cast an uneasy glance down at it, I wondered what my wife would say about a prolonged visit from my friend let alone the arrival of a second unknown person who required overnight accommodation.

"A man called Anton Drexler has written to me. He is the leader of a political party in Munich, and he wants to consult with me about a new member of his party. He plans to arrive in London tomorrow morning and to leave as soon as he has seen me. I think he is hoping I will join him on the way back. That is why my bag, at which you just gave a wary look, is of the size that it is, as I may go straight to Germany with him, and need clothing for a week. I cannot see any circumstances under which Herr Drexler would look to stay here."

I smiled at the ease with which Holmes had read my thoughts about his bag but there was still much I did not understand.

"And the consultation is about *German* politics?" I asked, for anti-German feeling remained very strong in this country only just over a year after the end of the fighting in Europe and less than eight months after the signing of the Treaty of Versailles. I would be a liar if I denied regarding anything German with only the deepest suspicion.

"Beyond what I have said, I fear I know nothing, but I can see no harm in listening to what he has to say. His letter was very insistent."

At nine o'clock the next morning, the tall, bespectacled, and moustached Drexler sat before us looking only slightly wearied from his journey. He had the air of a junior clerk, and I wondered whether a man such as this could really be the leader of a major political party. As my readers will know, Holmes spoke excellent German, and I had some knowledge of the language as well, so the discussion that I set out below took place largely in that language.

"I founded the German Workers' Party in January of last year," began Drexler. "Our membership consisted largely of railway workers, and I am myself a fitter on the Deutsche Reichsbahn or the German Imperial Railways."

"Pray continue."

"We meet weekly in one of Munich's numerous beer halls and discuss how to deal with the disastrous situation in our country following the calamitous decision of our leaders the year before last to agree to an armistice when our army was still undefeated in France, and then to sign the Treaty of Versailles in June last year."

Neither Holmes nor I ventured any comment at this.

Drexler then went off on a lengthy and somewhat rambling monologue about what he and doubtless many other Germans saw as the iniquities of the Treaty. It had resulted in the loss of a seventh of German land to create countries such as Poland and Czechoslovakia which had the support of the great majority of their citizens although not of their significant German-speaking minority populations, payment of vast reparations to countries Germany had invaded, and restrictions on Germany rebuilding its armed forces having, with its Central Power allies, sent its armies to conquer Luxembourg, almost all of Belgium, a third of France, and a large part of western Russia.

Drexler referenced all of this in what he said, and I omit any details for the sake of brevity as neither Holmes nor I made any response. He concluded as follows.

"Our leaders were at best – at best, Mr Holmes – fools, or at worst – and that is what I fear of some of them, Mr

Holmes – traitors to our nation. What was agreed has resulted in stringencies in Germany which you will not believe in the comfortable world you occupy here. People died of hunger because your blockade of our ports continued for eight months after the fighting stopped."

"There was a long period of food rationing here too because of the activity of your country's U Boats which engaged in unrestricted warfare and sank neutral shipping," I countered, feeling I had heard enough of Drexler's complaints.

"Children are growing up malnourished,"

"In France and Belgium, children were among the victims of your army," I countered again. "No foreign army was ever on any German soil."

"And our streets are littered with the wounded and the dying."

"If you did not see similar on your way here from Victoria Station, it can only be because you were not looking," I responded.

I think Drexler realised he had said as much as he could about his sense of injustice, and he fished a diary out of an inside pocket and studied it.

"Party member Adolf Hitler first came to a meeting of our party on the 12th of September of last year and he has been to every meeting since."

"He sounds a very dedicated member of your organization," said Holmes, "but I hardly think that that merits you coming all the way here to tell me about him."

"Mr Holmes, he seems to be in the process in the shortest space of time of taking us over. My fellow party members seem to hang onto his every word."

"So he seems to have the makings of a future…" here Holmes broke off, looking for the correct word in German and I broke in.

"Führer?"

"Thank you, dear Watson, yes, Führer, or leader to your organization is the word I was looking for. Is your concern, Herr Drexler, really about your own position in the party you founded?"

"My party's beliefs are bigger than any one individual," said Drexler looking defensive.

"Surely that is the point of any political party. Its core beliefs remain constant even if its members change. Members who are no longer convinced by the party's objectives, leave. The leader of the party is the person who can best articulate those core beliefs to attract voters."

"What is concerning me is that having started as a small grouping of fellow workers on the railways, our membership is suddenly growing rapidly, and our principal attraction is member 555, Adolf Hitler. Yet no one knows anything about him. He never talks about his life or what he has done in the past. It appears he lives only for the party."

"My dear Herr Drexler, have you read the numerous works about me by my colleague here?"

"I was not aware, Mr Holmes," said Drexler earnestly, and at this point he blinked at us quizzically through the thick lenses of his glasses, "that there were people who had not read your colleague's works about you."

"Then you will know that in the hundreds of pages of writings he has published about me, I have disclosed to him of myself no more information than that I have a brother, that I studied at a university which I have not named, and that I have produced monographs about a diverse range of subjects such as the tracing of footprints and the ash of different cigarettes. If your only concern about Herr Hitler is that he seems to have sprung from nowhere and that he is boosting the fortunes of your party, I remain unsure why you have made the long journey to London."

"There is something about him, Mr Holmes," said Drexler suddenly sounding plaintive. "He has an intensity of expression, of argument, and of gaze which is quite unlike anything I have seen in anyone else." He broke off once more and stared into the distance. "It is his staring eyes that disturb me most," he added after a pause.

"How does your colleague support himself? He cannot have a paid position within the party if it is as small as you say."

"I do not know. As I said to you Mr Holmes, he appears for our meetings but otherwise I know nothing further about him."

Holmes thought again.

"Does his accent betray no origin?"

"It is southern German," said Drexler after some thought, "but I could not be more specific."

"Do your party records not have an address for him?"

"We asked him about this, and he mentioned a place called Braunau, but then said he would pick up any party mail for him when he came to our meetings."

"Where is Braunau?"

"A town called Braunau is the German equivalent of a town called Brownfield. There is a Braunau in northern Bohemia, which is now in Czechoslovakia though which was until recently part of the Austro-Hungarian Empire. It is German-speaking. And there is Braunau-am-Inn in the newly constituted Republic of Austria. It is on the south side of the river Inn where it forms the border between Austria and Germany."

"So, based on his reference to Braunau, which may be the one in Austria or the one in Czechoslovakia, is he even a German citizen?"

"I do not know Mr Holmes," said Drexler, a note of defiance coming into his voice. "Austria wants to unite with Germany but is prohibited from doing so by the treaty of St. Germaine. To our east there is a large German-speaking minority placed against its will in this new country of Czechoslovakia. Self-determination, you will note, is not something allowed to German speakers although it is granted to everyone else in Europe. You will therefore perhaps understand that I have no idea of which country Herr Hitler is a citizen."

"What does he look like?" pressed Holmes.

"He is about one metre seventy centimetres tall, has what we call a toothbrush moustache because of its shape, and dark brown hair combed into a parting from the right. He is always dressed very smartly."

"So, he has fought on what you call the Western Front as he will have trimmed his moustache into that shape to fit it under a gasmask and there was no use of gas by the Russians in the east." Holmes paused for thought. "But I fear the information you have given me about him does not enable me to deduce anything else about him."

"You already seem already know than I do, Mr Holmes," said Drexler. "I merely know that he seems to dedicate all his time to the party."

Holmes remained silent and then asked, "If Hitler is party member 555 and your party has grown rapidly since he became a member, it cannot be all that small."

Drexler went once more back on the defensive.

"Hitler was in fact the fifty-fifth person who paid to be a member, but we gave out sequentially numbered membership cards starting from 500 to make ourselves look bigger to people who might want to join."

"So how many members does it have now?"

"We are anticipating two-thousand people for our meeting at the Hofbräuhaus at the end of this month."

Holmes was, I think, quite startled by this figure.

"Herr Drexler, are you saying that having had only fifty-five members in September, your colleague, Herr Hitler, has attracted nearly two-thousand new members within five months."

"They attend our general meetings," said Drexler, again looking a little uneasy, "but they are not necessarily all members although attendance at our meetings implies they are considering membership. Nevertheless, our numbers are now such that we need never have made use of the subterfuge of starting our membership card numbers at five-hundred to make ourselves look much bigger than we in fact were."

Holmes sat back in his seat.

"I think, Herr Drexler," he said at length, "with the support he has attracted in such a short space of time, and the air of mystery about him, your party member Herr Hitler merits an investigation. I will come with you to Munich."

"I am very pleased to hear it."

"Watson, would you care to join us? I am sure there must come a point when your practice can spare you."

The case Holmes was pursuing had seemed so speculative, and the demands of my practice were at that time so exacting, that I felt inclined to turn down the invitation, but Drexler interjected.

"If Dr Watson could act as a chronicler of what you find, Mr Holmes, that would, I am sure, be most valuable for posterity."

Eventually I agreed to put the practice in the hands of my two assistants, while I joined Holmes and Herr Drexler in Munich.

As Holmes had predicted, Herr Drexler returned to Germany on the day that he had arrived. I went through the process of handing over my practice to my assistants for an undefined period while Holmes spent the next day reading all that he could find about Germany in the reading room of the British Museum and at the National Newspaper Library.

With the whirl of events, it was evening of the second day, as Holmes and I were sitting at the hearth, before I had the opportunity to challenge him on his decision.

"I am not clear, Holmes," I said, smoke rising vertically from my pipe, "why you took on a commission which, if successful, can only strengthen the Germans, with whom we were until so recently at war."

"I confess, Watson, the same objections crossed my mind, but I have always found it to be a valuable use of time to investigate what our continental cousins are up to and, if it is a matter of statecraft, I can always refer it to brother Mycroft."

The next day Holmes and I, much like old time, crossed the English Channel and on Thursday morning we were in Munich where we took quarters at the Bahnhofhotel, which was, as the name suggests, a short walk from the main station. Even on that short walk, it was obvious that however many wounded and gassed soldiers there were in London, their numbers were multiplied two or three times in Munich. Many sat in ragged uniforms begging on the pavement.

Holmes had telegraphed our plans to Drexler, and he joined us for a late breakfast.

"We have a committee meeting at seven o'clock in a private room of the Sterneckerbräu beerhall on Sterneckerstrasse this evening," he said. "On his past record of attendance, Herr Hitler will be there – indeed I would be astonished if he were not. If you like Mr Holmes, you might sit with Dr Watson in the public area of the hall. Hitler will have to pass through it to come to our meeting and on his way out. I will meet him at the front door of the brewery and walk in with him so you can see who he is. Maybe, Mr Holmes, you can follow him after the meeting to see where he lives."

So it was that a quarter to seven saw Holmes and me sitting on either side of a long table in the Sterneckerbräu.

We had bought tankards of beer which we sipped on very slowly and avoided talking to each other as we were not at all sure how our fellow-drinkers might react to the sound of English being spoken. At just before seven, we saw Drexler walk through the hall in the company of a man matching the description of Hitler that he had given us. They disappeared through a door at the back of the hall. I am sure Drexler saw us, but he gave no signs of doing so. Holmes and I carried on slowly sipping at our drinks and at about a quarter past nine the man I knew to be Hitler came back out through the door, this time on his own. After he had walked past us, Holmes rose quietly and followed him, and I saw first Hitler and then Holmes walk through the street door and into the Sterneckerstrasse. I slowly drained my beer and returned to our hotel.

I sat up in our room and at a quarter past eleven Holmes came through the door.

"Well," said he, as he sat down and lit his pipe, "I don't know whether that was ever going to be all that hard. Hitler headed eastwards from the Sternecker and I was able to follow him easily. Munich is quite a compact city and to the east of it are barracks and that was where I saw him go."

"Were you able to follow him in? Surely there would be a gate and a sentry."

Holmes looked as evasive as Drexler had sometimes done.

"In a country as ruined as this one," he said in the end, "poorly paid sentries are amenable to a bribe, and I was able to persuade the guard to let me in without any difficulty. Hitler went into a building marked Offizierkasino."

"Hitler is a gambler?"

"Offizierkasino is the German for the Officers' Mess. The building was lit on the inside and there were no curtains. I saw Hitler through the window in conversation with another man in a uniform with insignia on it indicating he is a captain – so a senior person on the site."

"The other person may of course have nothing to do with Hitler activities in the German Workers' Party."

"I think that is unlikely. After a quarter of an hour, I saw Hitler leave the Officers' Mess and go to quarters marked Gefreiterschlafsaal or Corporals' dormitory. Hitler had thus come straight from the meeting of the Deutsche Arbeiter Partei committee to the Officers' Mess and then gone to bed in his own non-commissioned officers' quarters. I find it hard to believe that he was not debriefing his senior officer on the proceedings of the meeting when I saw him in the Mess."

"What will you do next?"

"Tomorrow I will get business cards made up for us and we will present ourselves at the barracks as two journalists from *The Times* reporting from Munich. We will see whether we can get an interview with the officer I saw."

Eleven o'clock on the next day saw Holmes and me presenting our false business cards – John Smith and Peter Brown – at the sentry box guarding the barracks. I think the sentry was surprised that anyone with a British background should be at a barracks on the edge of Munich but, once Holmes had greased his palm, he agreed to arrange for us to be taken to the most senior man on site and we were soon presented to Kommandant Karl Mayr, of 6th Battalion of the Guards Regiment in Munich."

"Not, you'll understand, that I anticipate doing any soldiering work any time soon," he said after introductions. "I've always thought that the more the British understand about us, the easier it will be to sort out an accommodation acceptable to all, so I will speak to your newspaper as long as it is off the record."

Holmes nodded his assent and Mayr continued.

"My main activity here is that I am head of the government's Education and Propaganda Department."

"What does that mean?"

"I suppose it means several things," said Mayr looking at Holmes and me in turn. "As you are no doubt aware, Mr Smith, the armistice and subsequent treaty are rejected by many in Germany, and we have not yet entirely stood down our army although what we have left has a completely different role from what it had eighteen months ago. We need to keep an eye on the population who are restive after a war which required great sacrifice for no gain, and we need to keep our troops employed – how usefully I am not sure matters. So soldiers here are paid forty Reichsmarks a month which is a good wage when all their living needs are also found. We will be demobilising our remaining soldiers at the end of March."

"Pray continue."

"I send our troops out anonymously to keep an eye out on what is going on. Since the armistice – we never refer to it as a capitulation though that is what it was, as we were out of ammunition and out of food – political parties have sprung up like weeds in Germany. Nationalists, Bolsheviks, socialists, democrats, social democrats. I don't think the members of the parties understand what half the terms mean."

"So your troops watch proceedings at these new parties and report back to you?"

"That is so. I get more reports than I know what to do with – generally one account of events is madder than the last. Blaming all politicians, the Kaiser, failure of the people, the mutineering sailors, the British not understanding us, and allies ratting on us."

"And what is your view?"

"In my present position, my opinion is unimportant. We have the politicians that we have, the Kaiser is gone, the people are the people and will not put up with starvation rations forever, the sailors mutinied when they were sent on a suicide mission, the British understood the Kaiser only too well, and our allies surrendered because they were in a worse state then we were."

"Do your soldiers not come to agree with a lot of the opinions they hear expressed at these meetings?"

"I do not know how I can keep track of what they think even if I saw a purpose to trying to do so. They are not supposed to participate in the workings of the parties they observe but I cannot in fact stop them. That will not matter either once we reduce our army to one-hundred-thousand men by the end of March. In reality, the observation work that they carry out is to keep them occupied although obviously I do not tell them this. I would be surprised if none of them agreed with any of the many opinions that they have heard at all these political gatherings."

The meeting went on, but Mayr had given us a reason why Hitler might be at meetings of the Deutsche Arbeiter Partei, why he might say nothing of himself to other party members, how he might support himself, and why he might take up political activities. Holmes soon brought discussions to an end.

"So, he is a spy! That is why he says so little about himself!" exclaimed Drexler when Holmes set out his findings to him. "He is not even a true believer." He paused, "And yet he is the reason why people come to our gatherings. His oratory has them all spell-bound. I cannot understand how he can have such passion when he is no more than a stooge."

"Might he not have been convinced by the arguments of your party."

Drexler thought for a minute. "I am not sure that the arguments of our Deutsche Arbeiter Partei are so different from those of many other parties," he replied in the end.

"He would not come to every single one of your meetings and take an active part in them if he were not convinced by your party's arguments. I should like to come to your next meeting and observe him at work," said Holmes. "You said you would have two thousand people there."

"Our next meeting is the one I referred to at our first meeting – so next Tuesday. Two-thousand people is our expectation based on recent meetings organized by our party but there may be more people or fewer. Hitler has not said he will attend but it would be the first time he failed to appear if he did not come. I am sure that you and Dr Watson could slip into the crowd in Hofbräuhaus unnoticed, Herr Holmes," said Drexler.

Holmes spent the next few days reading every newspaper he could find while I divided my time between walking the wintery streets of Munich and making the best sense of my own studies of the newspapers. So it was that at seven o'clock on Tuesday the 24th of February, Holmes and I joined what were huge queues outside the brewery.

We eventually got inside and sat down on two of the last seats still free at the end of one of the long tables. The other people in the hall were a mixture of the not very well-to-do – men in soldiers' uniforms, factory workers in overalls, and a large number of women. We watched as the crowd kept on coming in. Soon every seat at every table and then every other spare space in the hall was filled.

And yet there was no sign of the objective of our quest.

Speaker after speaker stood up and made speeches which sounded lacklustre to or, perhaps to be more precise, sounded to me as though they were being delivered by Anton Drexler. The material they contained was all the same – the Treaty of Versailles, the traitors in Berlin, the impossible obligations placed upon Germany. But the speakers were all reading from scripts, they repeated themselves, they tripped over their words, and I felt no sense of any of them gripping the audience.

I was beginning to wonder whether Hitler was going to appear at all when the main door to the hall was flung open. A drummer stood in the threshold and then walked in playing a slow, regular, insistent tattoo.

As though transfixed the hall fell silent.

The drummer continued with the same steady beat which rose in a crescendo.

Following the drummer and flanked by uniformed men came Herr Hitler who walked with a quiet determined tread through the hall and to the head of the hall where the speakers had been addressing the throng from a podium. But suddenly the podium was empty and, as Hitler mounted it, it was lit by a spotlight just as the hall fell dark, which meant that nothing else could be seen.

I have been asked numerous times since what listening to a speech of Hitler was like and I struggle to find an answer.

My German was capable of understanding what he said, and I set it out in the next paragraphs. But I had to look up in newspapers to find the content was, for it was how he said things rather than what he said that overwhelmed. The only thing I can compare it to is the speeches of the apostles after Pentecost. The apostles, filled with the Holy Spirit, spoke to the crowds assembled in Jerusalem who came from every country known to the writer of the Acts. And each member of the crowd seemed to hear the apostles speak in their own tongue. The result was that three thousand Jews from both inside and outside Jerusalem were baptised on the same day.

"Fellow party members," Hitler began, "we are a people awakening. You may look around and think how few we are. But we in this party are the core of the people. It is but a few short months ago that we had a mere handful of members and now here we are in the thousands. But we knew then, and we know now that our ideas are to be the only ones with any following in the land, that we want to be the sole power, and that we are only at the beginning of our journey."

"To reflect this, we must move on from being the Party of German Workers. We must be a party to the nation and a party of the people. We must become what we are – the party of nationalism and of socialism. I propose that we adopt the name the National Socialist German Workers Party."

This reads like a minor change of regulations – that the party of German Workers would be nationalistic and socialist seemed to me to be barely worth saying – but, even in the short passage I have quoted above, Hitler had captured the hearts and minds of the crowd, and the change passed by acclamation.

Hitler continued.

"At present we live with leadership that passes constantly from one group to another. We must replace it with a fixed pole of people of the best blood. Our goal must be that all loyal Germans become nationalists but only the best of them – we who are gathered here – become party members. We must be swift as greyhounds, tough as leather, hard as steel."

Again this aspiration, which reads as vague at best, captured the mood of the hall, and the crowd broke out into frenzied cries of "Vivat!" and – the first time I heard this – "Heil!" or "Hail".

"It is my destiny, so help me God, to lead this party," – again more acclamations – "and I will do so. We do not believe in the restraints of democracy, but we are in the best sense of the word a popular movement doing what the people want. There will be those who oppose this – the socialists, the Bolsheviks, the communists and the like."

This comment was followed by loud boos and Hitler went on, "But they are all controlled by our enemy – that race-tuberculosis of the people, the Jews, for it is they who control our press."

This sudden shift to blaming the Jews for all Germany's difficulties raised the pitch of the crowd from enthusiasm to hysteria. Hitler went on to announce a policy of excluding Jews whom he described as a pestilence from German citizenship and banning them from ownership of newspapers. He went on to announce no fewer than twenty-three other policies for the party. I do not believe anyone but an orator with a complete hold over his audience could have set out a list of such length and retained their attention let alone have each announcement met with cried of frenzied support.

He concluded his speech by declaring himself the sole leader or Führer of the party, a proposal which attracted roars of "Ja!" and "Heil!" There was not a word of opposition from anyone.

By the end I was deafened by the roars of the crowd and Holmes had gone white with shock. I am not sure I looked all that different. "When we got back to our hotel room, he sat in silence. All I could here was his intake of breath as he drew on his pipe. He did not say another word to me until we had crossed the Channel and were on our way back to Victoria.

"I fear, good Watson," he said at last, "that I have failed Drexler whom I believe to be an honest although limited man. And I fear I saw nothing in what Hitler said that would not appeal across Germany. He has a charisma, a forcefulness, and a magnetism that will attract people in huge numbers. Yet his control over his audiences is not something that is subject to reason and so I know not what I can do. It is obvious that Mayr has no interest in controlling him even if he were able to and Drexler has after last night already been sidelined. Hitler has been elected the head of the party by acclamation, and he will govern it by decree."

"What will you do?"

"When it is a matter of state, I defer to the judgment of Mycroft. Holmes glanced at his watch. "By the time we get back to London, it will be five-o'clock in the afternoon and Mycroft will be at the Diogenes. Let us go there and see what he has to say."

All was as Holmes had stated and we sat before Mycroft (whom I shall normally refer to as Mycroft to avoid confusion with his brother Sherlock) in the Stranger's Room.

Holmes set out what we had seen, and a look of quite unwonted concern came across Mycroft's features. He sat for several minutes in thought before he eventually spoke.

"Sherlock," he said, "you have gone so far as to describe me as *being* the British government. It is not for me to comment on whether this is an accurate description, but you will understand that *being* the British government means that my ability to interfere in German internal affairs is somewhat circumscribed."

He sat again for a while longer and then said in a voice almost as though he were speaking to himself. His tone sounded almost like a lament.

"If this were in England, it would all be so much easier. I would send in tax inspectors to investigate the affairs of Hitler's party, or wait until Hitler committed some infraction and offer the judge at his trial a place in the House of Lords in exchange for a suitable sentence. Or I would offer Hitler or some of his people some worthless honour or a constituency with a large majority so that they could sit in Parliament and go native. All these options are denied to me here."

He thought again.

"Well," he said at last, "I suppose Ludendorff might be…" he paused once more as he sought the right word, "…biddable."

It was only one and a half years since the fighting stopped, but I had already forgotten who Ludendorff was.

I think Mycroft saw my look because he explained, "Erich von Ludendorff was, along with Paul von Hindenburg, in charge of the German army in the war just ended. Immediately after the fighting had stopped, we had a military attaché in Berlin, Neill Malcolm. I got Malcolm to feed Ludendorff the line that the German army had been undefeated in the field but betrayed by the home front. Malcolm passed on the thought that the Catholics were suspect because their main loyalty was to the Pope, workers were suspect because they wanted a revolution like the Russians had, and that the Jews were suspect because the

British had promised them a nation of their own in Palestine."

"Was any of that true?" I asked.

Mycroft considered for a moment.

"I think Ludendorff was rather sold on the argument that everyone apart from him was responsible. Neill sensibly refrained from making the rather obvious point that if all the workers and all the Catholics were against Ludendorff, he could hardly claim to have national support. And we British have not delivered on any promise of a Jewish homeland in Palestine although the promise, caveated as it was by the wholly unrealistic wish for Palestine also to be the homeland for everyone else who lived there, was undoubtedly useful for getting the press in the United States on our side."

Mycroft paused again.

"In the end Ludendorff formulated it that the German army had been stabbed in the back. That was certainly rather easier for him to accept that than that the army which he had led had been defeated in eastern France, that they could not supply that army because strikes meant they could not bring arms across the Rhine, and that we could bring more troops to the battlefield than they could even though they had defeated the Russians."

He paused and took a pinch of snuff.

"So, Ludendorff was able to absolve himself from blame and we could get on with negotiating a peace without the risk of him claiming that the fight could be continued. He dedicated himself to writing his memoirs in which he valued his own skills very highly. If you read them, you will be surprised, given the views that he expresses in them about his own work, Germany contrived to lose the war at all."

"So how can Ludendorff help you?"

"We have done him a favour. People believe his word and he is thinking of re-entering public life. Arranging some success for him – some relaxation of the terms of the Versailles Treaty which he could claim as being his own doing is the obvious one – would increase his appeal among the people. I think he wants to be German president and something like that may be the way to help him."

I waited for Mycroft to go on, but he had come to an end of what he had to say and sat Buddha-like with a glazed expression on his eyes. In the end Holmes and I left him in his thoughts and my friend returned to his cottage in Sussex.

If this were a normal account of events involving my friend, I would now write about how Sherlock or Mycroft Holmes, or conceivably both, gave effect to Mycroft's plan. Hitler would in some way be rendered harmless and this country would have some sort of accommodation with Germany that both nations could accept – the Holmes brothers had a unique record of being successful in stratagems such as this. In fact, I can only relate an episode that happened nearly three years later and, although, it bears the hallmarks of a plot, I cannot be sure it was in fact instigated by Mycroft as he disclosed his schemes to me only when he thought I had a need to know what he was doing.

Accordingly, what I write below is what I have read in the newspapers.

On the 8th of November 1923 Hitler staged what became known as the Beer Hall Putsch – a popular uprising against Germany's Berlin government or the "criminals of November" as he put it. Hitler and Ludendorff and a group of National Socialists marched through Munich where they were confronted by armed police who opened fire killing sixteen of Putschists. Ludendorff was unhurt, Göring was wounded in the groin, and Hitler dislocated his shoulder. All three were arrested and put on trial for high treason four months later but Ludendorff was acquitted, Göring was freed because of the time he had already spent in custody, and Hitler was sentenced to five years but served only fifteen months. At the trial, the chief judge addressed Ludendorff as "Your Excellency," and the observations of journalists who witnessed the trial were that the judge was not opposed to the objectives of the putsch.

I cannot but wonder whether Mycroft had tried to organize matters so that Hitler was shot by the police in his putsch attempt, and that Ludendorff should become German leader, but that the difficulties under which Mycroft operated – working in a foreign country with forces over which he had far less control over than he would have had here – simply proved insurmountable even for him.

As it was, Ludendorff subsequently stood to be German president but attracted few votes. The man who became president was Paul von Hindenburg. It was Hindenburg who had dubbed Hitler "the Bohemian corporal" even though, as we subsequently found out, Hitler came from

Braunau in Austria not Braunau in Bohemia and was an Austrian citizen, and hence the name that Hindenburg devised for him was a misnomer.

Note by Henry Durham, historical advisor to
The Redacted Sherlock Holmes

Anton Drexler (pictured left) took no part on the Beer Hall Putsch and never held a senior position in what became the National Socialist German Workers Party or NSDAP after Hitler had become its leader.

Drexler was an alcoholic and died of complications arising from his addiction in February 1942. In 1933 President von Hindenburg had made Hitler Germany's chancellor or political leader.

On the death of Hindenburg, Hitler staged a referendum uniting the posts of president and leader and by doing so assumed dictatorial powers over Germany with results that readers will know all too well.

A Benefactor of the Race

Perhaps the works I chose to allow to be published in my lifetime fail to do sufficient justice to my friend's prowess as a scientist.

In our very first meeting, as recounted in *A Study in Scarlet*, he was in the process of identifying a re-agent precipitated by hæmoglobin and nothing else; this discovery was to be of inestimable value in subsequent police investigations. In *A Case of Identity*, he identified a substance as bisulphate of baryta as well as identifying the missing man who had been the subject of our client's petition. But other than these two isolated matters, I disclosed nothing about his scientific accomplishments. I even forbore to reveal that in 1878, thus several years before we met, an element had been named after him. Holmes was a mere twenty-four years old at the time and this made him the youngest person ever to have an element named in his honour. But he said nothing to me of his discovery of Holmium, and, as he himself told me when, as this work relates, I surprised his secret, it was at his own insistence that all books of reference stated that the element was in fact named after the city of Stockholm where he had worked in the late 1870s.

Pursuit of honours of any sort never motivated him and he declined offers of a knighthood in both 1895 and 1902. In the work that follows, my readers will now discover, he was also nominated for a Nobel Prize. Many will assume this will have been for his elimination from this life of Professor

Moriarty in 1891 for which deed a grateful world might have petitioned the Prize committee to award him the Peace Prize. But Nobel Prizes did not exist until 1901 and so my friend's chance of becoming a Nobel Laureate for that humanitarian benefaction was by then gone. The matter which I recount now relates to the Nobel Prize for Chemistry, and, as one might expect, it was in the end a matter of his own choice, that he did not become a Nobel Laureate.

It was on Thursday the 12th of October 1905 that our client, a small bespectacled man with a shaven head which made him look older than a man born as recently as 1868, entered the little sitting room in Baker Street. As so often when he had no case on, Holmes was engaged in one of his lengthy chemical experiments and he was holding to the light a test tube out of which a greyish-green smoke emanated as our visitor entered.

"My name," sad our visitor in a strong German accent as he presented himself to Holmes, "is Professor Fritz Haber. I have a matter of the greatest importance which I would wish to discuss with you."

"It is always a pleasure to meet a fellow-scientist. Is it about your science or is there another subject on which you would wish to consult?"

"I am unsurprised, Mr Holmes, that you can identify my scientific background although I can see nothing about me that would disclose it to you."

"Good sir, a splash of acid on the back of your left hand, a circular crease round your eye allied to a stooped gait from looking down a microscope – it would take a dim observer indeed not to classify you as a scientist and almost certainly, like me, a chemist, although I could not from that evidence alone surmise in which branch of the science you specialise."

"Very well, Mr Holmes, it is about my science I would wish to seek your advice."

"Then pray do so."

I expected Professor Haber to set out a narrative of experiments, formulae, Bunsen-burners, and test-tubes. Instead, our visitor seemed more interested in Holmes's biography, and he looked at my friend closely as he started.

"I have read in the works of your colleague Dr Watson here, that you have written monographs on topics as diverse as the art of tattooing, the tracing of footprints, and the polyphonic motets of Orlando de Lassus."

"That is so."

"You do not, if I may make so bold as to say so, extend your range of publications to topics of interest which have a non-specialist following or which may be of benefit to more than a limited section of society."

"I write on subjects that are of use to my work and that are of personal interest to me," said Holmes after a pause for thought.

"Quite so. Your colleague," here Haber nodded at me, "has at one point in your collaboration – I believe it was in *The Red-Headed League* – described you as a benefactor of the race. I, by contrast, feel that much of your work is, as your brother opined, related to petty matters of the police court."

"My brother Mycroft's specialism is omniscience. I, by contrast, am omniscient in specialisms," said Holmes, I think slightly nettled by our strange visitor's apparent dismissal of his work. "For a forensic investigator such as me, it is the little things that are infinitely the most important."

"My work, by contrast," said Haber, leaning back in the chair to which Holmes had directed him, "is of key interest to the whole of mankind. Indeed, it is not too much to say that the further spread of mankind may depend on its outcome."

"Pray continue."

"Have you ever wondered what a world without hunger might be?"

Silence.

"Surely," our visitor, his eyes widening and acquiring a gleam I found disconcerting, "something that would end want, disease, ignorance, squalor, and idleness would be something you would wish to investigate. In *The Naval Treaty* you have described the board-schools as lighthouses and beacons of the future turning out hundreds of bright little seeds from which will spring the wiser, better England of the future. But a lighthouse throws a narrow beam, and the horizon limits the distance from which a beacon may be seen. What I have in mind will be transformative for the whole of mankind."

"Pray continue," said my friend again, I think intrigued, as I was, as to where this was leading.

"Crops such as wheat, rice, and potatoes, which are the staples of what we eat, benefit from nitrogenous matter in the soil which stimulates their growth. If they lack nitrogenous matter – if, for example, the soil has been exhausted of nitrogenous matter by previous crops of a similar type on the same piece of land – then the crop yield is liable to be paltry. Between a third and a quarter of agricultural land lies fallow at any one time and much other land is deemed unviable for use in agriculture because it is insufficiently fertile."

Silence.

"Has it struck you how peculiar it is that when we live on a planet whose surrounding atmosphere is 80% nitrogen, nitrogenous matter should so often be wanting for agricultural production? But if some of the atmosphere's abundant nitrogen could be provided to plants in a form they could use, then crop yields would increase exponentially and human hunger would greatly diminish. A diminution in human hunger can only result in a diminution in human conflict as title to fertile land will assume a smaller importance in human affairs."

"But as a chemist," objected Holmes, "you will know as well as I do how hard it is to get atmospheric nitrogen to combine with anything at all let alone to get it into a solid form that will increase the fecundity of crops. Air itself is a mixture as the nitrogen in it will not compound with the oxygen with which it is mixed."

"I have been working on a means to make nitrogen more liable to compound. I have found that if I extract hydrogen gas from methane, and mix it with atmospheric nitrogen, put it under pressure, subject it to a high temperature, and put it in the presence of a suitable catalyst – that is a material which facilitates a chemical reaction without at the end of the reaction being changed by it – I can produce a reaction which delivers ammonia in the form of solid compounds which can then be used as a fertiliser. But the scientific processes and materials are complex and dear and thus the process I am seeking to initiate is not commercially viable in its present form."

"Your work with temperature and pressure are clear to me," replied my friend, now looking keenly interested. "May I ask what catalyst you are using?"

"I am using osmium."

"Osmium?" asked my friend for the first time in our acquaintance sounding unsure when a matter of science was being discussed. "My files, good doctor," he added without even troubling to turn to me and deploying the disembodied voice he used when deep in thought. Indeed, as he said it, I noted that his eyes were three-quarters closed as if he were in a trance. I found osmium between entries for Osmiroid, a venerable manufacturer of writing implements, and osmosis, a term for the movement of liquid from areas of different concentrations through a semipermeable membrane so that the concentrations at the end are equal in both areas.

Osmium, I discovered, was one of the rarest metals on earth.

"It is sixty times as expensive as gold," said our visitor when I mentioned his preferred catalyst's costliness, "and is only isolated as part of the extraction of platinum. I started my experiments with platinum which is a metal often used as a catalyst. Platinum is itself very expensive, but I found that the even costlier osmium had better results."

"What is it you wish me to do?" asked Holmes.

"You are one of the minds of the age. I have a laboratory at Karlsruhe in south-western Germany which can offer you every facility for your investigation. For work such as this, there will be no constraints of time or money or of any other sort to your work. You may use whatever materials you want and there are devices which will allow you to raise those materials to a temperature or to apply to them a pressure only constrained by the current laws of physics."

Although in the works I allowed to be published in my lifetime I never dwelt on the matter, by 1905 the reward of no less than £12,000 that my friend had received for finding Lord Holderness's son in 1903, had rendered Holmes financially secure and he could take or leave work as he chose. I quote him exactly when he now said, "The opportunity to be, what my colleague Dr Watson in a piece of characteristically purple prose, calls a benefactor of the race of man is one that is hard indeed to pass up. I will give the investigation the concentration it merits."

It took my friend not many minutes more to pack his portmanteau for an extended absence and then he was gone. Over the months that followed, we were together but little. Occasionally I saw him if he returned to London for a particularly complex case and sought my engagement. Otherwise, as far as I was aware, he was as focused on his scientific work as he had been twenty years earlier in the matter which opened *The Reigate Squires* in which for two months he never worked less than fifteen hours a day, and had more than once, as he assured me, kept to his work for five days at a stretch.

My readers will also be aware that it was around this time I married for a second time and moved out of Baker Street to Queen Anne Street a few hundred yards away where I had bought a large practice. The dwelling from which I worked was a substantial one and ran to large grounds unusual even then in central London. My predecessor had previously neglected his house and his practice for the plot around his house and his garden were extensively planted. As a result, the house was full of builders and to maintain both the house and grounds in a condition in which I could accept patients, I was obliged to keep a large household – a butler, a cook, several maids, and a head-gardener with associated under-gardeners quite apart from the staff I needed to run my practice."

It was in early 1910 that I received a telegram from Professor Haber. It simply said, "Mr Holmes ill. Come to Karlsruhe at once."

Ah, how a plea to see my friend tugged at my heart!

In a few minutes I had closed my practice down for an undefined period, packed my bag, said a hurried farewell to what was a growing family, and was on my way to Victoria for the boat-train. The next day saw me in southern Germany where Professor Haber met me at the station.

"I fear your friend has over-exerted himself. He is raving and has been confined to hospital. He needs a doctor who understands his peculiarities and that person could only be you which is why I summoned you."

I confess I was not sure what to expect and when I got to the hospital it was to find Holmes heavily sedated and, to my horror, the subject of physical restraint though he wrestled ferociously with the fetters that bound him. Under his breath he could be heard muttering terms from the laboratory which would only have much meaning to an expert – retort, bell-jar, compound, mixture, suspension – and babbled about temperatures at levels in the hundreds of degrees and pressures many times that which is normally encountered.

"He has over-taxed himself," said Haber soberly. "I have never seen a man work so long and so hard."

I confess I had half hoped that Holmes was merely acting as he had at the time of *The Dying Detective* but fleeting touches to his fevered brow and pounding pulse were all I needed to assure myself that this collapse was genuine. I stayed with him round the clock for several days making sure that he had complete peace and, as the raging fever passed, I was able to secure a place for him at a nearby sanatorium. It was several weeks before I deemed him fit enough to return with me to London and even then only on condition that he came to live with me at Queen Anne Street.

The exchange that follows is a summary of discussions that Holmes and I had over his time in hospital, in the sanatorium, and on the train back to England. "Even replicating Haber's result with osmium was a struggle. The yield of ammonia was miniscule and would never be commercially viable. I applied more heat, less heat, catalysts of all types." A long pause and his words seemed to be being dragged from his body. "More pressure, less pressure." Another long pause. "More catalysts. On their own, in compounds, and in mixtures. Sliced, diced, powdered, extruded. I confess I was tempted to resort to the world of necromancy – work when the moon was at the full, when it waned, with a four-leaf clover, or with a rabbit's foot in my pocket. None of my base metals turned to gold." Every so often, as though in a daze, he would come out with the line, said almost as if a prayer, " 'Oh say not the struggle naught availeth, that the labour and wounds are in vain'."

And things were even worse when Holmes was at Queen Anne Street.

He sat for days at a time saying nothing as he stared into the distance. He even stopped smoking and turned down flat my every plea to take it up again. He reacted in the same way to my attempts to fortify him with brandy. In the end I felt it incumbent on me to smoke more in his presence to ensure he got a suitable amount of tobacco into his lungs. I was tempted to add a dose of brandy into everything he drank but I feared that his sense of taste would see through the ruse and my deceit might lead to a permanent rupture in our friendship.

At a loss as to how I might succour my friend, I arranged for his violin to be brought from Baker Street and this was the one thing that seemed to cheer him and quite contrary to his normal practice, he sat playing airs from Gilbert and

Sullivan's *Pirates of Penzance.* Under his breath I could hear him mumbling the name of elements – I clearly heard antimony, arsenic, aluminium, before the rest faded out – as he played. As someone with a scientific background, I wondered why he arranged the elements more or less alphabetically rather than in the order of the periodic tables, but he stared straight ahead when I put to him questions on this point or any other.

As a next step I decided I would have to resort to remedies favoured by more modern practitioners such as taking my friend for walks in the park, circular breathing techniques, and the freshest food. This latter was easy to arrange as Jarvis, the head-gardener, had planted the garden entirely with peas and beans which were by now just coming into season. As the weather was wet, July saw a surfeit of these and even the imagination of my cook was hard-pressed to disguise that we were eating the same thing over and over again for all that it came straight out of the garden.

"More peas?" queried Holmes as we partook of a viscous soup one lunchtime which seemed to contain nothing else. These were the first words he had said for several day. When he followed this up with, "And even more beans," as a stew appeared consisting of broad beans, French beans, runner beans, haricot beans, kidney beans, and not much else, I thought a word with the cook might be in order.

"You want us to use what's in the garden, Dr Watson, and that's all there is," said Whitcombe. "Maybe you should ask the gardener why he planted what he did." Rather to my surprise, Holmes, whom in my assessment of him at the time of *A Study in Scarlet* I had described as having no knowledge of practical gardening, seemed to take an interest in what I hesitate to call my investigation, and together we went to senior gardener's shed.

"Your predecessor in this house, Dr Watson," said Jarvis in his broad country accent looking somewhat taken aback at having his work subject to questions, "had a passion for gardening greater than his knowledge. He planted it intensively and in doing so he all but exhausted the soil."

"But that does not explain why you have now planted nothing but peas and beans."

"I wanted to cover the ground with something. Peas and beans help exhausted soil to recover although only to a limited extent. I could have left the entire garden fallow but that would hardly look attractive to your patients when they come to call."

"You interest me exceedingly," chimed in Holmes sounding suddenly much more like his normal self. "Do you know why such crops have this effect?"

I think Jarvis was even more startled at being questioned by someone of the eminence of Sherlock Holmes than by his employer. In the end he came out with, "Dr Watson asked me to maintain the garden as I saw fit. I have been a gardener man and boy. When and where I learned the trick of planting peas and beans to restore soil, I have no idea now, and I have no idea how it works. I will plant them once more next year and after that the soil will have fully recovered so I can then plant anything I am asked to grow."

I turned to Holmes, "If peas and beans are converting nitrogen in the air into solid nitrogenous matter, it can have nothing to do with extreme pressure or heat. Surely," I said, and I confess a slight note of triumph came into my voice, as I said what follows, "if you exclude that impossibility as we have, what remains and so must be true is that they contain something that catalyses the process for….."

I broke off for before I could complete the sentence Holmes was already off running up the garden to the house. He had gone by the time I entered. "All I heard, Dr Watson, was the front door opening and closing," said Graves, the butler. "I fear Mr Holmes left no indication of where he was going."

I hardly wanted an official police investigation into the disappearance of my friend, but I was not sure where to search for him. I looked in at Baker Street thinking I might find him in his own personal laboratory, but Mrs Hudson looked at me blankly when I asked her as casually as I could where he might be and said, "I've not seen Mr Holmes for almost as long as I've not seen you, Dr Watson."

I could not search for Holmes in any haunts as he did not, to my knowledge, have any. It was of course always possible that he had made straight for Karlsruhe, but I had his passport at Queen Anne Street, so this struck me as unlikely. Another place with laboratory facilities he might have made for was St. Bartholemew's where I had originally met him two decades and more previously.

And there he was!

I could see how he had spent the hours he had been missing as, somewhat incongruously for the orderliness of a professional laboratory, he was surrounded by piles of bean and pea plants including the roots. It must have taken him some time touring market-gardens and nurseries to get them together in that quantity and then transport them there. As I entered I could see him in a corner with his back to everyone as he lent over a Bunsen-burner, but I was relieved to see a tendril of what could only be tobacco smoke spiralling up from over his shoulder as he worked. When he saw me, rather than giving me the hunted look I had seen in the previous days and weeks, he explained, "I came here to see how peas and beans fix nitrogen out of the air if that indeed is what they do. I suspect that Haber was unknowingly replicating something that these plants do, and your gardener said their effect on exhausted soil was limited."

But the St. Bartholemew's laboratory was really designed for medical experiments, and we were soon heading back to Karlsruhe. "At the very least, good Doctor, your comment on catalysts entitles you to a footnote in the history of a work that will make the world ring," Holmes said and so it was on his insistence that I accompanied him, and we were soon at the laboratory with Haber. The German scientist seemed at first to misunderstand what had brought us back to Karlsruhe. "You think you can extract osmium from members of the family *Leguminosae?*" he asked. "A patent on a process like that would make any country rich for if osmium can be extracted from plants, then platinum cannot be far behind."

"I had not conducted my experiments with that objective in mind," said Holmes looking slightly taken aback at the direction Haber seemed to want the research to take. "My aim was to facilitate the conversion of nitrogen from the air into nitrogenous solids and thereby increase crop yields."

"Indeed so, Mr Holmes," replied Haber soothingly. "At peaceful times like these a scientist belongs to the world not to his country."

My friend was to spend weeks at the laboratory analysing what metallic compounds were present uniquely in peas and beans and in the end further experiments revealed that iron augmented by oxides of calcium, potassium, aluminium, and silicon – all of these items thousands of times cheaper than osmium – would catalyse the reaction. It was not so long that with the facilities present at Karlsruhe, he had optimised what is now, as my reader will now realise is somewhat simplistically, known as the Haber process, and the result was twenty tonnes of nitrogenous material per day.

"I believe," exclaimed my friend to Haber, "that one should always say things as they are, and these results are of such magnitude, it is not too much to say that this will transform human existence as we know it."

"In der Tat, or indeed so," replied Haber. "So many things will now be possible which were previously inconceivable," although we were not to know at this stage quite what Haber had in mind.

My reader will know that it was not many years after the events described in the foregoing that for the first time Britain found itself at war with Germany.

Until 1871, Germany had been a geographical concept but not a unitary state. None of Germany's motley patchwork of minor kings, principalities, and dukedoms on their own or in any conceivable coalition could pose a threat to this country and its Empire. Thus there was no reason for a war. It was Prussian military domination that led to the unification of these numerous city states and provinces, and perhaps war between this country and Germany was inevitable as they competed for the world's resources. I have, in *His Last Bow,* referred to my friend's activities at the outbreak of that conflagration although my readers will already have learned in other works of my friend's involvement in major world events after the Great War which render the title of the work, *His Last Bow*, inaccurate.

The start of the Great War resulted in Holmes and me seeing more of each other than we had for nearly a decade. The British government – in fact his brother Mycroft, whom I shall refer to by that given name to avoid confusion with his brother Sherlock – employed my friend as a consultant on any number of projects and the two brothers often used my house as a base for meeting away from British government premises.

So it was in early February 1915 that I was advised by telegram that the two brothers were coming to Queen Anne Street for a top-secret meeting.

"It's like this," began Mycroft without preamble. "This war has been going on several months and is hugely costly in terms of manpower and material. I thought it would be over by Christmas because the blockade of German ports by our Navy stops them importing products such as saltpetre and guano for making explosives as well as preventing the import of foodstuffs which will cause widespread hunger and hence popular discontent. We must therefore assume that there has been some delay in their capitulation."

Rather to my surprise, Mycroft paused to mop his brow at this point, and I heard him murmur, "An uncharacteristic failure of judgment on my behalf. This must not get out." For my own part I wondered that he had really summoned his brother and me to a top-secret meeting with the objective of imparting to us the news that Germany was about to run out of materials to fight and that consequently the end of what had already been a horrifically bloody war was in sight.

I was about to give voice to this question when Holmes spoke in a tone lacking its normal assurance.

"I fear my assistance to Professor Haber," my friend divulged, "in turning atmospheric nitrogen into nitrogenous matter for fertiliser may help the enemy avoid the food shortages our blockade of their ports might otherwise have caused."

"Your assistance with what?" asked Mycroft, for the first time in my acquaintance with him looking discommoded. He put the back of his hand to his nose to take rather more than a few pinches of snuff and Holmes had to wait to repeat what he had said about his work on fertilisers with Haber.

"Well, Dr Watson was right when he described your knowledge of chemistry as profound and your knowledge of politics as feeble. So that is why the Germans can continue to produce explosives!" exclaimed Mycroft at last.

"Nitrates are a key component of dynamite and with their ports blockaded we thought that the Germans would soon run out of ordinance. Rather than being unable to import the material that they need to make explosives because their ports are blockaded, they are obtaining it from the process that you and your scientist friend, Haber, have pioneered. And your work is also having the effect of preventing a popular uprising among a hungry civil population." Mycroft glared at his brother and paused to take another huge quantity of snuff before he continued. "I expect the process will come to be known as the Haber-Holmes process. Congratulations brother, you have probably lengthened this war by four years."

"But Haber's interest seemed to be only to benefit humanity and to end human want. He said that a scientist's mind belongs to humanity."

"In peacetime, possibly. In wartime a scientist belongs to his country. As you are about to find out," retorted Mycroft before taking several more pinches of snuff. It was some time before he had sufficiently calmed down to speak again.

"Well, this makes what I wanted to talk to you about even more important. We fear that the Germans may, if they get desperate, resort to tactics illegal in the conduct of war."

"What might be illegal in the conduct of a war such as this which started with the violation of the neutrality of two countries, and which is producing thousands of casualties a month?" I asked in some wonder.

"Attacks on civilians. Poisoning the water-wells of enemy combatants. Or using poison gas on the battlefield. And that is what I came here to talk to you about, Sherlock."

"But surely," I interjected again, "the Germans would not be so foolish as to use poison gases on their Western Front as the prevailing winds are from the west. There would be a risk that the gases would blow back onto their own positions and retaliation from our side would be likely to be much more effective than any initial strike from them for the same reason."

"We may never be too sure about what desperation may drive the Germans to do and if they are foolish enough to be first users, we must have the ability to strike back. Sherlock, I wish you to develop gases suitable for use in combat and have them at the ready."

"I am only prepared to do so if I can be guaranteed that we will not be the first to make use of such horror weapons. The most obvious gases – chlorine and mustard gas – cause agonizing and lingering injuries as well as mass death."

"I understand, dear brother, that all is fair in love and war. While I, and I suspect you, have no knowledge of the first aspect of life in which fairness plays no role, I can assure you that in war fairness's role is very much circumscribed."

"I repeat, I will not be party to research into poisonous gases unless I am guaranteed that there is no first use on our part."

But Holmes's hand was forced when the Germans became the first belligerent to make significant use of poisonous gas in April 1915. British outrage was unconfined when we saw the victims of German gas attacks – young men bent double like old beggars under sacks, knock-kneed and coughing like hags, as war-poet Wilfred Owen was to put it – on London streets. By the end of the war, due to Holmes's efforts, we had produced about 25,000 tons of poisonous gases and I have no doubt that the German victims of British gas attacks looked much the same as British victims of German attacks.

My friend became emotionally charged by the horror of what had been unleashed in a way I had never seen before. "I worked with Haber to eliminate want, disease, ignorance, squalor, and idleness and instead I find myself creating it," he lamented. "And I cannot doubt that it is Professor Haber, much the foremost of German scientists and hence my German equivalent, who is behind not only the manufacture of explosives from atmospheric nitrogen but the preparation of poisonous gas attacks."

As Mycroft had anticipated, it was to be nearly four years before the war ended and the toll of casualties ran into the millions, hundreds of thousands of whom were due to the use of poisonous gas by both side.

It was in December 1918, a month since the start of the Armistice that ended the war, that Holmes asked if he could arrange an appointment at my house. I was ready as always to acquiesce, but my reader will share my astonishment that the person who joined Holmes and me was Professor Haber.

I was unsure of what to say – my practice at this time had been largely given over to dealing with the medical consequences on our troops of explosives and gassings –

and it was Professor Haber who opened the discussions although it was to my friend he addressed that he addressed his remarks.

"Mr Holmes, the process we devised with atmospheric nitrogen has met with such success that the Royal Swedish Academy of Sciences were in touch with me during the conflagration just ended and suggested that you and I are to be awarded the Nobel Prize for Chemistry. They see the award as a step towards reconciliation of our two great nations. I have been given special permission to come here and to invite you to Stockholm to accept it." Haber turned to me, "Maybe you too, Dr Watson, may get some share of it and you would be welcome to travel with us."

For me this was all too much.

"I cannot be a party to this, Holmes."

My friend, who had been even more taciturn than normal, appeared to be struck dumb and a long silence followed that was only broken by a knock on the front-door.

I took it upon myself to answer it ahead of the butler, relieved to be out of the presence of a man whom I regarded as an angel of death.

I was slightly less surprised to find myself facing Mycroft Holmes on my step than I had been to see Professor Haber. Behind Mycroft was Inspector Lestrade and two burly policemen. I had had Mycroft on my step too often before not to know that he would enter whether I wanted him to or not and stood to one side to let his party in. It was Lestrade who spoke first as the group entered my reception room.

"Professor Haber, I am serving you with an indictment as a war-criminal."

Haber was, I think, too astonished to speak.

"You may choose to remain silent but anything you say, will be taken down, and may be used against you in a war-crimes trial," added the inspector with the fine sense of fair play of the British law.

"I am a patriotic German who has done nothing but do his best to serve his country in a war that has now been lost," protested Haber in the end. "I do not see that killing a man with gas is worse than blowing him to pieces with a shell and, rather than this underhanded trap to arrest me, I would point out that when I was a combatant in uniform. I went to the front to make sure that my science was properly used."

"Your use of poison gases was against the Hague conventions."

"The French were the first users of poison gas when they shelled us in August 1914. It was only because the quantities of gas they delivered were so small as to be insignificant that we made no complaint at the time. It does not do to tell your enemy that his attacks are ineffective. Your attempt to indict me is only because due to my efforts we were able to succeed with the use of gas where the French failed – or at least they failed until the British made available to them the skill of Mr Holmes."

"This is no time for petty arguments," said Lestrade clapping his hand-cuffs onto Haber's wrists, and it was not many more minutes before Holmes and I were again alone.

"Haber wrote to me by the first post between Britain and Germany after the Armistice," said Holmes as if in explanation though his words seemed not to be being addressed to me at all

He paused to light his pipe before he continued.

"I confess I thought at the time that letting the letter through to me might be being used as a means to entrap him as I could see no other reason why his letters to England might come through, let alone, why he might be allowed to travel here. Mycroft *is* the British government, and he has proved his Machiavellian capabilities again here as an arrest in your reception-room is as discreet a place to spring such a trap as can be imagined."

The next I heard of Haber was in newspaper accounts of his journey to Stockholm to accept the Nobel Prize for his work on what might have been called the Haber-Holmes process but was to become known as the Haber-Bosch process, Bosch being another German chemist. To this day Haber remains the only person to be an indicted war-criminal and a crowned a Nobel laureate. And for all his process's use in making materials for explosives, it undoubtedly helped feed the world in the hungry years after the end of World War I when farmhands, farm machinery, and land free of mines were all in short supply. It continues to do so in every corner of the planet.

It was in 1924 that the two Holmes brothers stood once more on my doorstep.

"Professor Haber has written to me," said Sherlock Holmes, "seeking my help. He says that the reparations which the victorious allies have demanded from Germany…"

"With complete justice," I snorted. "The Germans laid waste to a third of France,"…

"…have led to a rise in dangerous political extremism which threatens the established order in Germany. Haber is looking for a way for Germany to meet its debts and has hit on the idea of trying to extract gold from seawater," continued Holmes.

I think this idea sounded bizarre to both Mycroft and me and there was a silence before anyone spoke.

"Is that not like," I asked, dredging memories of *Gulliver's Travels* up from my schooldays, "trying to extract sunbeams from cucumbers to provide heat and light on winter days?".

"Do not forget, good Watson," said Holmes with a slight hint of reproof in his voice, "that it was Haber's idea to try to use atmospheric nitrogen to make ammonium nitrate, a solid compound of nitrogen, hydrogen, and oxygen. Many might have considered that Haber's idea a conjuring trick no more implausible than what you have just described. As seawater is ubiquitous, it must contain traces of every element. The difficulty is to concentrate particular elements in commercial quantities."

"For my part I am not at all sure," mused Mycroft, "whether is a good thing or a bad thing that a country which has seen political turmoil ever since its defeat in 1918 should be faced by the overthrow of its established order."

He paused to take a pinch of snuff.

"I think on balance," he continued at length, "a stable Germany at the heart of Europe is preferable to an unpredictable central power bent on revenge for its defeat. Thus Sherlock, on mature reflection it would be in this country's interest if you helped Haber in his project. At this distance, I can see no way a positive outcome of the research could have negative consequences for this country and indeed your presence, dear brother, along with Dr Watson here, and this time armed with a degree of scepticism about Haber's motives, can only be a good thing."

When we eventually met Haber, he commented, "I got the idea, gentleman, from your identification of peas and beans as concentrators of nitrogenous matter perhaps by using a concentrate of osmium in the process. Let us see what we can do to concentrate the gold in sea-water."

Holmes showed the same dedication to the search for gold in sea-water as he had shown to fixing atmospheric nitrogen as into a solid compound and, amongst many other expedients, tried to catalyse the process with holmium, a metal almost as scarce as osmium. This was when I became aware of this element and its discoverer for the first time. But we made no progress.

My reader will know that German political developments at this time became more and more alarming although Haber, employed at this time by the Kaiser Wilhelm Institute for the Advancement of Science, remained sanguine about it.

"There are always hotheads who achieve a brief prominence and then disappear from sight when the impracticality of what they want to do becomes clear," he remarked as we met to discuss the disappointing results of our latest attempt to extract gold from sea-water. "But even as someone who is a Jew by birth, though baptised and not a great believer in anything other than scientific progress, I am sure there is nothing for me to worry about. Even as legislation is being considered to limit the role of Jews in public life and the professions, exemptions are being included so that these restrictions do not apply to people like me who served at the front in the war just past. I am sure this will all blow over just like everything else has done."

His dismissal from his position at the Institute as soon as the National Socialists came to power in 1933 was thus a huge shock to him and he was forced to go into exile. "I have had to leave all my work behind," he said to me on his way through London bound neither he nor I knew whither, "and goodness knows what use or misuse will be made of it."

He was to spend the next few months hawking his skills to various governments around the world.

He ended his days dying of a heart-attack in a hotel in Basel, Switzerland, in January 1934, on his way to taking up a post as director at the Sieff Institute in Mandatory Palestine.

Note by Henry Durham, historical advisor to *The Redacted Sherlock Holmes*

A third of annual global food production continues to use ammonia from the so-called Haber-Bosch process a hundred years after its invention and it supports nearly half the world's population.

For the reasons outlined in Dr Watson's account of events above, Haber is also known as the father of chemical warfare.

Amongst the other inventions of Dr Haber was Zyklon – a gas which was a cyanide-based insecticide.

A further development of this gas was Zyklon B in which Haber had no involvement.

Zyklon B was used in the Second World War by the Germans as part of their human extermination program.

I am indebted to Dr Malcolm Driver, scientific consultant to *The Redacted Sherlock Holmes* series, for his elucidation of the scientific aspects of this work.

A Certain Idea of France

I have referred in other accounts of events to which I was witness, how my friend, Mr Sherlock Holmes, and I spent the years of this twentieth century's second great global conflagration at Fenny Stratford near the mansion at Bletchley Park where, as I was eventually to learn, Holmes acted as a consultant to the code-breakers working there. Callers to our cottage were rare, but the ones who came were, almost without exception, of the most senior levels in the conduct of the war. Indeed, I would be guilty of an indiscretion tantamount to treason were I to disclose more than is strictly necessary to make the matters I present now and elsewhere in works on this century's latest great war comprehensible to the general reader.

There will be those readers who wonder what state of health Holmes and I were in by the 1940s, for the adventure that lay before us was to hold rigours that would have taxed many younger men. I would advise that throughout our acquaintance Holmes observed a regimen of the utmost asceticism. His staples were simple food, which was even simpler in wartime, and tobacco, to which he always seemed to have sufficient access to meet his health needs. My own regimen followed his after we once more came to share quarters after the death of my second wife in 1937. Thus, while in our advanced years our physical prowess was not what it had once been, our intellectual capacities were unimpaired, and we were both endowed with levels of mobility and robustness equal to the challenges that this adventure confronted us with.

It was in early May 1944 that there was a knock on our door.

On the step stood a tall man in a peaked cap who introduced himself as General Charles de Gaulle, leader of the Free French. I took him into our little sitting-room where he sat for some time without saying anything at all. Instead, he confined himself to puffing at a cigarette he had lit without asking – not, of course, that permission to smoke would have been withheld. The silence continued for some time, and it was only when Holmes himself opened his mouth to speak that de Gaulle finally gave tongue to his thoughts. "How," he asked querulously, "does one govern a country with two-hundred-and-forty-six different kinds of cheese?"

In all our long acquaintance, no client had ever opened a consultation with Holmes with a question anything like this, but of course Holmes had an answer for it.

"In these straited times, good sir, any kind of cheese is hard to come by, and, General, it seems to me you are still quite some distance from being able to govern anywhere at all as your country remains occupied by the Germans."

De Gaulle drew heavily on his cigarette, and sighed. "You are, *hélas*, right on the first point, Mr Holmes. On the second point, I am breaking no confidence when I say to you that an allied landing on the French mainland is planned for this year although I cannot disclose to you when or where. Accordingly, the German occupation of my country may end sooner than you imply."

My friend stayed silent, I think waiting for de Gaulle to present a specific problem, and de Gaulle continued although he seemed to be talking almost to himself.

"France is a powder-keg and has been since the Revolution – actually, the first of several revolutions – of 1789. If there is a successful landing and the Germans are driven out, there will be a power struggle amongst the competing political affiliations in my country. Besides the many Frenchmen who have fought against the Allies on behalf of the Axis powers, there are my own forces of the Free French, and there are the Communists. It is not at all inconceivable that the winners of that struggle will be the Communists. They have displayed the greatest bravery of all the political parties in the fight against the oppressor even though they initially opposed the war to defend Poland because the Soviets were among the aggressors against Poland. I do not believe it is in anyone's interests for my country to be run by the Communists or by people who have previously thrown in their lot with the Axis powers."

De Gaulle paused as though unsure of what to say next.

"Am I to take it, General," interjected Holmes drily, "that your preferred outcome is that it should be you yourself who holds power in France once the Germans have been expelled?"

"Throughout my life," replied de Gaulle, a far-away look coming into his eyes, "I have had a certain idea of France."

"As a politician?"

"I am a soldier," came the general's response. "Politics is too important for the politicians." Our visitor paused and then drew heavily on his cigarette before saying audibly but almost to himself. "La France, c'est moi."

"You mean you embody France?" asked my friend, not letting the mumbled comment pass.

"If I want to know what France thinks, I find it easiest to ask myself."

There was another long silence.

"My dear General," said Holmes, a slight note of asperity entering his voice, "Even in my advanced years, my time is of value. Are you able to be more specific on what it is you want to see me about?"

"I fear, Mr Holmes, I cannot. I have mentioned to you that there will shortly be a landing on the continent of Europe. The plan of our Allies is to land and to head eastwards through Belgium and into Germany."

"Surely that must be the easiest way to defeat the enemy?"

"It is to ignore Paris, the crucible of France. If the Communists establish a power-base in Paris, they will have an easy time establishing a government for he who controls Paris controls France. And yet our allies wish to leave Paris in the hands of the Germans, so the chances of a Communist takeover are high."

"I regret General that I cannot advise you on a military matter. My specialism is criminal investigation."

"Mr Holmes, you asked me to be specific on what I want from you, and, if I am honest, I have at the present time no clear idea. But you are one of the minds of the age. I would be grateful if I could avail myself of your insights to see if we can find a way to achieve a European settlement that meets my vision."

"Are not your objectives to liberate France and to defeat the Germans?"

"I am sure that would form part of my vision."

"And how am I to provide my insights to you when you will be fighting on the Continent?"

"I would wish that you and the good Dr Watson here form part of my staff. As leader of the Free French, I already have a small staff, and it would be my desire that the two of you be attached to it. Arrangements will be made to ensure that both of you are well-protected."

Holmes turned to me. "Well, Watson, what say you? Many years ago, I quoted Gustave Flaubert to you. 'L'Homme n'est rien. L'œuvre tout.' It would seem churlish not to put that saying into action now."

"Gustave Flaubert is saying that the individual is nothing, it is his work that counts," said de Gaulle for my benefit, as I struggled to translate from the French of which my knowledge had grown a little rusty in the half a century since Holmes had first cited the quote. "I remember well when you said it, Mr Holmes," continued the Frenchman, visibly brightening. "You quoted it in *The Red-Headed League*. And your knowledge of such a pillar of French culture as Gustave Flaubert confirms the wisdom of my choice in engaging you."

"I quote the German poet Goethe as well as Gustave Flaubert," objected my friend. "Indeed, I quote Goethe twice and Flaubert only once in the works published by Dr Watson here. I trust you have…?"

But our strange visitor was not to be deterred by what he obviously regarded as a trifling matter. With a shrug he took his leave saying as he departed, "I have an office in St James's in Central London, and I will see you there tomorrow. I will send a car to collect you and Dr Watson. Prepare to travel to places unknown and not to be back for the foreseeable future. If at all."

No more than a few minutes had passed, and Holmes had not expressed any comment on this vaguest of commissions that we had just received when there was another knock at our door.

This time on our step stood the Prime Minister, Mr Churchill, wreathed as ever in cigar smoke, and I ushered him into our little sitting-room.

Just like de Gaulle, he sat smoking for several minutes, before speaking. For the second time that morning, it was only when Holmes opened his mouth and was, I assume, about to ask our petitioner what he wanted that our visitor spoke for himself. "I suppose Mr Holmes, if I were to ask you whether General de Gaulle had been here, you would tell me, as you told Lord St Simon in *The Noble Bachelor*, that you extend to the affairs of your other clients the same secrecy which you promise in mine."

There was silence from Holmes and Churchill continued.

"Some, Mr Holmes, have compared de Gaulle to Joan of Arc. Alas, my bishops won't allow me to burn him at the stake much though I am often tempted to do so anyway whether I receive episcopal blessing for such an act or not."

My friend said nothing, and Churchill continued.

"De Gaulle is selfish and arrogant. He believes he is the centre of the world. He has a country house in a place called Colombey-les-Deux-Églises. I understand that in an uncharacteristic act of modesty, he permits that one of the two churches that give the place its name to be given over for the worship of God."

Churchill paused and a column of cigar smoke spiralled up towards the cottage beams before he continued.

"In this war it is the Russians who are providing the blood as they have the population and have been invaded, it is the Americans who are providing the money as they have it and without it neither we nor the Russians could sustain the fight, and it is the British who are providing the time needed for victory to happen and the place where American forces can be based. And the French? Well, they are providing a certain…"

He paused looking for the *mot juste* and, since Holmes was still studiously making no remark, I proffered, "Je ne sais quoi?"

"Yes, that is the expression I was seeking, Dr Watson," said the prime minister to me as he drew on his cigar so that its tip glowed red, and he continued. "although I had been hoping to hear the wisdom of Mr Holmes. To have as big an impact as de Gaulle when he has so little in the way of resources is an achievement not to be underestimated. Truly, General de Gaulle is a great man."

Still no word crossed my friend's lips.

"As you will not speak to me, Mr Holmes, I will leave you with a simple instruction which, as a free agent, I presume you may choose to ignore. Should the general come here and petition you, it is my wish that you should fall in with whatever he says. Indeed, you should do what you can to make his wishes come true however perverse you may consider them. I would do nothing to come between General de Gaulle and his wishes."

And with that, the Prime Minister was gone.

"Well, Watson," said Holmes, "a remarkable pair of petitioners if you can describe the disquisitions that they came with as petitions. I would have been happy to go wherever the general asked us to go without further ado, but an injunction issued without any explanation from our own Prime Minister that we do what we can to make sure that the general gets what he wants makes the commission quite irresistible. And we will be going back to London. It will all be rather like old times."

So it was that Holmes and I presented ourselves the next morning at 3 Carlton Gardens, a building that in happier times would have been rendered in white stucco but which now was painted a gloomy khaki to prevent it attracting the attention of air-raids.

De Gaulle was a whirl of energy as he greeted us. "We are off to Algiers," he said.

"Algiers?"

"That is where the French government in exile is."

"The French government in exile?"

"It is called the French Consultative Assembly."

"Who consults with whom and on what topics?" asked Holmes.

"I have no time to answer detailed constitutional questions such as that, Mr Holmes. That is the name that the assembly has been given, and Algiers is where it sits. We must away there now."

I will not detain my reader with the details of the weeks that followed as we travelled with de Gaulle first to Algiers, and thence to Normandy where on the 14th of June – so just over a week after the Normandy landings – he got a hero's reception in Bayeaux although I noted it that the French town was barely six miles off the Normandy beachhead. We went back to Algeria, and then in early July to Washington, New York, and Ottawa before we returned once more to Algiers. "I need to be in Algiers in order to be able to follow events," he explained but what he heard seemed not to satisfy him as on the 18th of August he suddenly declared, "We must *encore* to Normandie. We will fly to Casablanca, then to Gibraltar, and then onto Normandy."

After flights in which our trajectory varied between diving low to skip from wave to wave to avoid radar and soaring to the heights to dodge from cloud to cloud to avoid enemy fighters, we made it to Gibraltar. Here the fighter escort for our unarmed Lodestar broke down. De Gaulle insisted we continue in our now unescorted plane regardless of the increased peril that that involved, and we took off just before dark, flew west far out into the Atlantic, and then headed north towards the English Channel.

As we reached the parallel of Cape Finistere on the north-west French coast, a sou'wester broke. We could see a mounting look of panic on the face of pilot, Colonel de Marmier, as the tempest gripped our craft and shook it like a rag-doll. The noise from our engines rose to a scream as our plane fought the storm. We could watch our navigator plot our location on a chart which showed us being pushed further and further northwards although in the blackout we had no idea whether we were over land or sea.

Colonel de Marmier suddenly turned to us and said something in French.

De Gaulle uttered what sounded like an expletive and started to rage at the pilot.

"I told him that by the mercy of God, the storm has driven us over England," said the pilot pleadingly to Holmes and me in heavily accented English. "In this weather, we must take the opportunity to make landfall here. We are almost out of fuel to get there."

"We must to France," barked de Gaulle at the pilot. "Dès que possible! As fast as possible!"

"Pas possible."

"La France, c'est moi," I heard de Gaulle mutter, and he pulled his pistol out of his pocket and pointed it at de Marmier, shouting. "Si vous m'obstructez, je vous liquiderai!"

For the next few hours, I watched as the fuel gauge headed down towards zero, but maybe the storm abated, maybe the pilot had overstated the danger, maybe the wind blew in our favour, but eight o'clock the next morning saw our engines cut out just as we sighted an airstrip. We glided down to land on a bumpy stretch of grass near Bayeaux.

"'Si vous m'obstructez, je vous liquiderai!' is the only piece of French I have ever heard Mr Churchill use in all my dealings with him," said de Gaulle, suddenly mildness itself, as the plane came to a composed halt. "I own that he considers that I have obstructed him quite often and that consequently he has threatened to liquidate me quite often," he added as we descended from the plane.

"But why are we here?"

"The Americans have broken out of their beachhead. They are heading into Brittany. The right-hook they are calling it. Now is the time to...," but he broke off and I saw a man in American uniform walking across the grass towards us.

Soon de Gaulle, Holmes, and I were in the operational headquarters of General Eisenhower where we were joined by General Omar Bradley of the American First Army and General Leclerc, which was a name completely new to me. "My real name," said the soft-spoken, moustached Frenchman, introducing himself, "is Philippe Leclerc de Hauteclocque. But I am known by the name Leclerc to protect my family which is still in France. I am commander of the second division of the Free French." A French major named Gribius stood guard outside the tent.

As though to emphasise how much the matter meant, as soon as we sat down de Gaulle took up with Eisenhower where he had broken off with us above, "Now is the time to make a dash to Paris and free it."

"We have discussed this before," responded Eisenhower, with the wearied air of someone who was reiterating something already long settled. "My responsibility is to the American people and to the American president. If we go and liberate Paris, not only does it mean that we are diverted from chasing the Germans back to Germany as we will be thrusting south rather than east, but we will end up having to feed the citizens of Paris and there are four million of them. That's four tonnes of food and fuel a day and my supply lines are stretched as it is. It is lack of supplies that has kept us from breaking out sooner. The way things stand, the Germans will have to feed Paris."

"You think the Germans will continue to feed a population of four million people if you bypass Paris?" asked de Gaulle.

"The Germans seem to have kept France reasonably fed during their occupation. We have found no cases of malnutrition in the areas we have reconquered. As I have said before, I can't sanction the risk of American lives to gain something that would only be of trophy value."

"You are saying Paris is only of trophy value?" exclaimed de Gaulle, outraged. The arguments circled round without any sign of a breakthrough, but Eisenhower was unmoved.

In the end de Gaulle sighed and said, "General Eisenhower, I am too poor to bend the knee. My army has now made landfall here, but it has been in exile for several years, and we have no material of our own. I will ask Mr Holmes here to make the argument that Paris should be liberated *dès que possible*."

I am not sure that Holmes was expecting to provide his advice on a matter of military strategy, but he asked for maps of the frontlines to be brought before us.

"Generals all," said Holmes at last, looking round at the assembled company, "if we stick to our plan to thrust eastwards, there will be a major German force in Paris to the south of the line of advance which can disrupt both the troop movements of forces heading east and the supply lines to keep those forces provided. The capture of Paris would neutralise that. Does it not therefore make sense to give that priority?"

There was silence round the table and, sensing he was at an advantage, Holmes pressed it home.

"And if the necessary equipment were given to General Leclerc's Free French to make for Paris, would the danger to American lives not be eliminated?"

Eisenhower turned to Bradley and said, "What the hell, Brad, I guess we will have to go in now that a proper military argument has been made for it."

De Gaulle turned to Holmes. "And it will be the French who are liberating Paris. Mr Holmes, I would wish that you and Dr Watson accompany General Leclerc here," said he pointing to the man sat next to him.

Not many minutes more passed, and we were walking out of Eisenhower's headquarters. As we came out into the sunshine, Leclerc cried to the major standing guard outside, "Gribius, mouvement immédiat sur Paris!"

In 1895 our next move in the adventure would have been to descend the seventeen steps down to Baker Street and spring into a hansom bound for Victoria Station and thence make to the City of Light. In these strange times "mouvement immédiat" meant a delay of several days as the second Free French division was geared up, and it was not until the 22nd of August that we were ready to advance.

"The front line of our forces," said Leclerc as we headed south-east, "needs to get to the west bank of the Seine about thirty-five miles from Paris. We will have to cross minefields, and we will have to assume that every building on the way is booby trapped." Thus, progress was slow, and it was not until it was just getting light on the 24th of August that we stood at the river-bank. There was nothing to indicate the other side was defended but, as we stole up to the water's edge, Leclerc nudged Holmes and whispered.

"We have just received a radio message that there is a delegation representing the Paris Resistance waiting for us on the other side."

"How have they got there?"

"I do not know but they will not have got there without the Germans letting them through."

Signals were exchanged across the grey water and eventually we heard the sound of paddles as a contingent of Resistance fighters led by a man who we were told was the brother of the Swedish ambassador rowed cautiously across the river and stood before us.

"The Commander of German forces in Paris will see you," he said.

"It's a trick," growled Leclerc sceptically. "The Germans are looking for more time to prepare their defences."

"It is we who need more time to build our resources," a small grubby looking member of the Resistance replied. "We would not entertain this communication otherwise. We are not yet ready to stage an all-out assault. Our ammunition is low, we have no heavy weapons, and we have no imminent prospect of supply."

In the end it was agreed that Leclerc, Holmes, and I should go to Paris under German escort.

Various formalities had to be gone through and, once we had crossed the river, we were blindfolded.

I am not sure what regular readers of the activities of my friend would make of the sight of Mr Sherlock Holmes sitting in a vehicle covered by German military insignia. That, however, was the situation in the early gloom of that August day as we sat in a German staff car for an hour until we were told we had arrived at the Germans' Paris headquarters. I was later to learn that this was at the Hotel

Mercure on the banks of the Seine, but I had no means of knowing this at the time. Soon we were before a pudgy, monocled man in a field-grey military uniform who was seated behind an imposing desk.

"I am General von Choltitz," he declared to us in a heavily accented English as he lit a cigarette. "I am Wehrmachtbefehlshaber or supreme army commander of greater Paris."

"Although only a recent arrival," observed Holmes.

Chlotitz looked startled at Holmes remark but before the German could say anything, Leclerc butted in, I think anxious not be overshadowed by the presence of my friend. "I am General Leclerc."

"I confess," said von Choltitz to Leclerc, "I have never heard of you…"

"My name is not exactly my own," murmured Leclerc. "I …."

"I was going to say, I had never heard of you under that name. Do not think I do now know your real name or where your family lives," snapped von Choltitz, disregarding the Frenchman. He turned to look at Holmes and me. "But you," he said, "must be Mr Sherlock Holmes and Dr Watson. Those are names that any man of my standing must be proud to have dealings with. I understand, Mr Holmes, that you are a member of the elite French Légion d'Honneur."

I think Leclerc was put out by von Choltitz's attitude towards him and interjected before Holmes could respond,

"We are here to accept the surrender of Paris to the Free French."

"Really? And on what basis would that be?"

"We have an army massed thirty-five miles from here and we will overwhelm you if we have to. And the Resistance here in Paris is poised to strike."

"I confess, dear General, I am not really sure why I am seeing you at all," drawled von Choltitz. "I have a well-trained and well-equipped garrison of many thousands of men. And I have instructions from the Führer to hold Paris to the last man and to destroy it if it cannot be held. He took up a piece of paper that was on the desk in front of him and read, 'Paris must not capitulate. If it cannot be held, it must pass into enemy hands as a field of ruins.' Those are my orders, and I have mined all of Paris's bridges and major buildings. If your troops move east of their current positions, the whole lot will go up but not before many men will have been needlessly killed in street fighting which will also damage or destroy large parts of the city."

He paused and was about to continue when we were interrupted by a knock.

"Herein," said von Choltitz.

"Der Führer am Apparat," said a young adjutant, who was sweating heavily.

"Stellen Sie ihn durch," instructed von Choltitz. "It is the Führer calling me," added von Choltitz to us. "I have asked for him to be put through and you might as well stay while

I speak to him. I do not imagine our conversation will be long."

Von Choltitz's desk-phone rang and von Choltitz picked up.

"Ja, mein Führer."

After many years of neglect, my German was rusty, but I knew enough to understand the repeated shouted iterations down the telephone of, "Brennt Paris?"

Von Choltitz spoke calmly down the phone.

To my surprise, he even walked to the window as far as the phones cable would go and held the receiver out into the August sunshine before walking back to his desk. I heard the hoarse shouting down the telephone's receiver switch from, "Brennt Paris?" to "Der Verlust von Paris bedeutet den Verlust von Frankreich," but after saying a few more words, von Choltitz replaced the handset onto its holder.

"As you may have understood, the Führer is asking if Paris is burning," he said to us. "I told him that there are no signs of an insurrection and that everything is in place to torch Paris if the need arises. He was saying that the loss of Paris means the loss of France."

I think von Choltitz was waiting for one of us to say something but neither Holmes nor Leclerc said a word and in the end it was von Choltitz who broke the silence.

"When our troops first moved into the Soviet Union, we were greeted by enthusiastic crowds in Kiev and Minsk. People were pleased no longer to be under the authority of the Russians and gave our troops gifts of flowers, bread, and salt. We might have had a better result in the Soviet Union if we had tried to keep the people sweet there. Here in France, that is what we have done, and we have peace. Not a single German soldier is stationed here because of the activities of the French Resistance which shows you how seriously we need to take them. They are all here to defend the sea-board. In Germany we say that the good life is to live like God in France. If you move on us with your American supplied weaponry, I am sure many French people would flock to our side in preference to being taken over by the disorderly Anglo-Saxons."

"You think the French would fight on your side?" asked Leclerc.

"We have had far more French fighting on the side of Axis than there have been French fighting for you. Do you really think we have held a country as big as France for four years without any sort of disturbance if we did not have the people on our side? If there is a fight, there will be fighting from street to street and between brother and brother. There is no willingness to fight among more than a tiny minority of the French."

There was a pause, and I waited for Leclerc to speak but he was struck dumb. Eventually it was von Choltitz continued.

"I have also organized a truce with the Resistance. I had worked out by how rarely they shot at us how low they were on ammunition, and I suspect they wanted time to regroup. Meanwhile I am keeping Paris running as normally as possible. There are race meetings on, the cinemas are showing films, and the circus is in town. All three entertainments are being watched by enthusiastic crowds who have no interest in seeing their city being destroyed in battle."

"Will you surrender this city?" reiterated Leclerc, urgency in his voice, "If you do not, we will seize it anyway."

"For the reasons stated, I do not think you will find it at all easy to seize Paris," drawled von Choltitz. He sat back in his seat awaiting our next gambit.

I felt the parleying had some way to go. In the end it was von Choltitz who spoke next.

"I am prepared to let Paris be a closed city if you route your troops round to bypass it, and head eastwards into the teeth of our defences to the north of here. We will do what we can to keep the city going. But gentlemen, if you attack me, the Eiffel Tower will go up and so will Notre Dame. It is no worse than what British and American bombers have done to cities in Germany."

I still felt that von Choltitz was biddable but was not clear where the discussion would go next.

"And if I surrender Paris, Hitler has introduced *Sippenhaft* for his generals," added von Chlotitz.

"What is *Sippenhaft*?" asked I.

"My wider family bears the punishment for my actions if I am not myself in German custody. I have a wife and three children so you will imagine my concerns. It is a barbaric measure worthy of the Middle Ages." He turned to Leclerc. "You may rest assured, your wife and children are safe and well in their village near the Belgian border. For the moment."

We had reached an impasse.

"My observation while blindfolded in your staff car," interjected Holmes, "is that we will find the city much easier to take by force than you are saying if in the end we are left no choice but to do so. You may not even have time to mount a defence if our army moves. And if the city is destroyed you will be held responsible."

He paused.

"What might make you change your mind, General? I am thinking about your personal circumstances."

Holmes posed this question with the air of a man laying down a trump card.

Von Choltitz started at my friend's words. Holmes opened his mouth again, I think, to reveal how he had made his deduction but, before he could do this, von Choltitz broke in, his words tumbling over each other as he did so.

"With you, Mr Holmes, I will deal. You clearly have a better grasp of the realities of the situation than anyone else."

He reached into an inside pocket of his uniform and pulled out a piece of paper.

"I have a statement that I would like Mr Holmes to sign although I suppose you may do so as well, General Leclerc. It says that I handed Paris over to the French when I was in a position to defend it. For this act of clemency, I would like indemnity for my actions in all this war's theatres. The document also specifies I must not be placed in French custody."

"Are you now saying you will not defend the city? My men are up for a fight," said Leclerc taken aback.

"So," summarised Holmes, "General Leclerc wants to take Paris by force if necessary and General von Choltitz needs to make a show of a fight to protect his family…?" His voice trailing off as we all realised that a deal was possible.

"I am sure some of the troops here will fight," said von Choltitz, suddenly all eagerness. "There is a strongpoint at Palais de Luxembourg which is manned by members of the Schutzstaffel."

"What is the Schutzstaffel?"

"Schutzstaffel is the full name of the SS. They will not take orders from the Wehrmacht, and I fear how they will react when news of the surrender of Paris has been announced. It would gladden my heart if there were a set-to between them and your Resistance."

"Who are itching to prove their mettle," said Leclerc eagerly. "But this document must be signed in any case by the French," insisted Leclerc. "It is the French who are rising and recovering their capital city. I insist we sign this to move the matter forward."

"As I said, General, if Mr Holmes signs it, then I am sure you can sign it too," said von Choltitz with a shrug.

Leclerc shrugged in turn. "We can have Paris. The British can have you."

He signed with a flourish and passed it to Holmes who was reluctant to sign but in the end did so, I think mindful of Churchill's instructions to fall in with whatever de Gaulle wanted, and the Germans surrendering at Paris could be seen in no other way.

It seemed slightly unnecessary in the circumstances, but Leclerc then produced an instrument of surrender which von Chlotitz signed without bothering to read.

"When General Paulus signed the surrender at Stalingrad," he said as he signed, "my former colleague said that it was a personal surrender, and that he could not undertake that his troops would stop fighting. I will do what I can for you to make sure our troops stop fighting."

"Now my troops will go to take out the Palais de Luxembourg to sort out your strongpoint," replied Leclerc.

"The strongpoint is hardly mine anymore but, if I may say so, with the city surrendered it seems hardly fair not to offer the troops there a chance to surrender."

I could see that Leclerc was torn between the desire for a bloodless end to the drama and for a chance for the French to show what they were capable of. In the end the four of us headed to the Palais de Luxembourg where a cease-fire was arranged.

"I thought we were trying to protect Paris," exclaimed von Choltitz when he saw how damaged the Palais and the surrounding streets already were, but he went inside, and emerged shortly afterwards.

"I have no command over the troops, but they said they can run through their ammunition in an hour, and come out. For my part I have told them that they will not have protection under the laws of war after that."

I confess I thought the hour that von Choltitz had organized would be a formality and that no one would want to carry on the fight when a time for the end to hostilities had been set. Instead firing from both sides continued with unabated ferocity right up to the end of the stipulated time. Many of the hundreds dead amongst the French and the Germans in the liberation of Paris happened after von Choltitz had signed the instrument of surrender, and the mercy was that deaths were not in the thousands.

It was not many more hours after that that von Choltitz, Holmes, and I sat in an American Jeep driven by a member of the Free French heading north.

Holmes asked von Choltitz if he would like a cigarette.

"I recall," replied the German, "that you offered Count von Bork a cigar in *His Last Bow*, but he declined to accept it. For my part I would be delighted to have a cigarette."

Holmes passed von Choltitz a cigarette and lit it with his own.

"I have always been a soldier among soldiers, Mr Holmes," said the German, as the tip of his cigarette turned red, "but here I have had to play a role more akin to that of the sort of tightrope walker now at work in one of Paris's circuses and even that greatly understates the complexity of my part."

"Pray continue."

"A tightrope walker can only fall to the left or the right. And there is normally a safety net underneath. For my part,

I have had more directions to keep my balance on than there are points on the compass."

"Kindly explain."

"I had to put on a show of force to keep the Resistance in awe of our power, so I had my troops marching through Paris to demonstrate their might. I had to put on a different sort of show to the general population of Paris and gave them bread and circuses to stop them rising up against me and making the situation uncontrollable. And I had to keep the fact that these measures were tactical devices secret from the forces of the enemy and yet make sure that any aggressive measures were visible to my countrymen so that no moves be taken against my family."

"And with what result?"

"The truce held, Parisian shops remained stocked, the circus ran. I avoided using the wireless to tell the population of Paris of the truce. Instead, I had announcements made on loudhailers and on leaflets dropped from the few aeroplanes I had so that no word would be broadcast to my masters in Germany of what I was about. The Free French can now make the most of their defeat of our last strongpoint so that the world including the Germans will think that they freed Paris by force on their own."

He paused and puffed at his cigarette.

"Can you explain your behaviour, General?"

"Can you explain how you deduced my defences were weak?"

"That was simplicity itself. We got from the front line to your headquarters in what I could see was the centre of Paris in less than an hour. A well-prepared defence would have required numerous stops at security posts and a circuitous route."

"I feel like your friend Dr Watson here when a deduction is explained to him! You were also right to deduce that I had only been in Paris a short time."

"It was your German matches that told me that. Had you been in Paris for any length of time, you would have been using French matches."

"Again, I feel like Dr Watson here," said von Choltitz amiably and he went on. "I arrived in Paris on the 7th of August having been sent there by the Führer. I had gone to see him still full of hope that the miracle weapons would bring final victory and found instead a man who seemed only able to harangue and yet who was so hollowed out by events that his harangues made no impression. He trembled as he spoke, he was bathed in sweat, and became more agitated and rebarbative the longer he spoke. There had been an assassination attempt a few weeks previously but a man who is not capable of leading should not be leading and I came to Paris charged with the desire – well the desire neither to die nor to destroy the City of Light."

"What will happen to your family?"

A shadow came over von Choltitz's face.

"I do not know. They are torturing and hanging those who launched the assassination attempt a month ago and their families are being locked up. But," he said, brightening, "the wife of Field Marshall Paulus of Stalingrad is still at liberty, and that gives me some hope. And now I will be held by the British with this letter signed by Mr Sherlock Holmes saying that I will not be prosecuted for anything I have done. For my own part I cannot imagine a more trustworthy document."

Just as my friend was about to speak, von Choltitz broke in again.

"I am a soldier. I get orders. I execute them." He paused and my sense was he had something of moment to impart. In the end he continued, not meeting the eye of either Holmes or me, "In a war one is given orders. And I acted in accordance with those orders in the Crimea even though the orders were sometimes against the laws of war. The worst thing I had to do, though I carried it out with great thoroughness, was the liquidation of the Jews after the capture of Sevastopol. And now, who knows, Mr Holmes. I may end up being a member of the Légion d'honneur just like you. Perhaps in the end I will become known as the Saviour of Paris."

Von Choltitz face had borne the most haunted expression when he started speaking but by the end of the disposition I have quoted above he looked quite chipper.

By contrast, an appalled look came over my friend's face at von Choltitz confession and the subsequent jest. Had he been younger I am not sure how he would have reacted to it, but, as it was, he confined himself to turning his face away from von Choltitz, and addressed not a word to him or to me for the rest of the long journey.

We get back to London on the 27th of August. Von Choltitz was taken into custody and Holmes headed straight for Downing Street where he was told that Mr Churchill was in Paris. There was nothing else to do but to head to Fenny Stratford where Holmes sat slumped in his chair too limp to do anything other than smoke.

It was on the 3rd of September that there was a knock on the door, and I was soon welcoming a cheerful looking Mr Churchill into our sitting room.

"You have really done remarkably well, Mr Holmes," said Churchill, as he sat down. "It has all worked out rather splendidly. Paris has been neutralised, de Gaulle rather than the Communists is at the helm, and the Germans are being chased out of France."

For the first time in our dealings with Churchill on this matter, my friend spoke to him. "On our way back to England, von Choltitz boasted of massacres he had carried out in the Crimea. And I had signed a document saying that no war-crimes charges should be brought against him for action in any theatre of war."

"Did the French agree with that arrangement?"

"They did not disagree, but they were only small players in the great events."

"If the French signed, then you may set your mind at rest about it."

"But von Choltitz was admitting to a massacre."

"I have had to do things that I would not normally wish to do. I have ignored a famine in Bengal which has killed millions. I have signed up to a bombing campaign against German cities which serves no strategic purpose other than to create misery as German cities are clear of both population and war-industry. And its true import is that when this war is won and we have conquered Germany, the country we will come into will be a land of ruins which will make dissent and guerrilla action far harder to eliminate. If that were not enough, I am also in the process of agreeing to boundaries in Eastern Europe that will lead to the displacement of many millions of people whose only crime was to be the victims of German aggression."

Churchill leant back in his chair and the tip of his ever-present cigar glowed scarlet before he continued.

"If required to choose between Europe and the open-sea, I will always choose the open-sea as it is there that the route to being a great power lies. If forced to choose between the Americans and the French, I will always choose the Americans as it is with them that the people of these islands enjoy a special kinship. I have a certain idea of France, and I am happy for it to be its own somewhat deflated version of a great power. I would not wish a similar deflation to happen to us. I expect that the French will want their own zone of occupation in Germany and that will reduce the burden of administering Germany on this country. And I would not be at all surprised if the French, the Germans, and others will, after this conflagration is over, want to set up some sort of United States of Europe. But that is of no interest to this country and its Empire, for we will always have much bigger fish to fry."

For the first time, Holmes posed Churchill a question.

"If you and de Gaulle want the same thing, why did you come here to ask me to make sure he got it?"

"Because Mr Holmes, as you have demonstrated, you can deliver to a commission in a way not possible to a lesser mortal. And, if I am honest, because if de Gaulle knew that he and I wanted the same thing, then I am sure it would have made him want something different, and he might then seek to trespass on the ambitions of this country. Either the Germans or the French will always be the dominant power on the western Europe continent, and it is my preference that it be the French and that they concentrate their energies on that. De Gaulle is the one man in France who might deliver something different."

A few more puffs of his cigar though no more words and the Prime Minister was gone.

It was perhaps inevitable that only a few minutes later it was General de Gaulle who took his place in our sitting room.

"Has Churchill been here?" he asked.

There was silence from Holmes who sat smoking staring straight ahead while I repeated the refrain, "My colleague extends the same degree of secrecy to you as he does to all his clients."

De Gaulle seemed untroubled by this and addressed my friend.

"I mentioned to you Mr Holmes that I have all my life had a certain idea of France. We are a power fit to take our place at the same table of victors as the Americans, the Russians, and the British. Eventually the conflicts in Europe will be resolved and Europe will look for leadership. I expect that it will look to France."

"Do you not think Europe will look to Great Britain for leadership after we have remained the only European belligerent not to be occupied by the Germans and played the fullest part in Europe's liberation?" I asked as Holmes stayed silent. For my own part I was taken aback by the self-assuredness of a man who had spent four years entirely dependent on the British for his safety and support.

"Dr Watson, if I am candid," came the reply, "I do not regard the British as European. It will be France which will provide Europe's international power once it is allied to German industrial strength."

"You see France in alliance with Germany? With the Germans still occupying parts of France?" I asked.

"I see Europe being led by a German horse being ridden by a French jockey. I would seek to exclude your country from any such arrangement. Your country may follower its vision of being a global power and flirt to its heart's content with a somewhat uninterested America."

"But large parts of France are still in German hands and many of its cities are as much a ruin as the cities in Germany. How will it be able to become a great power?" I countered.

"France cannot be France without its grandeur. We will do what needs to be done to achieve and maintain that grandeur."

De Gaulle soon departed without Holmes having said another word and it was not until November 1947 that I have had a chance to pen these words.

De Gaulle became President of France in 1944 but fell from power the next year just as Churchill did in this country. No war-crimes charges were ever brought against General von Choltitz who has just been released from custody. I understand he is to join his wife and family in the French zone of occupation where he will write what I am sure will be highly profitable memoirs as a prelude to enjoying an easeful retirement.

Note by Henry Durham, historical advisor to
The Redacted Sherlock Holmes

This is not the first time that the heated relationship between Winston Churchill and Charles de Gaulle has been brought to public attention. This is, however, the first time that the fact that both consulted with Sherlock Holmes and Dr Watson in 1944 has been disclosed and it will be news to many that the post-Second World War settlement in Western Europe which rather excluded the United Kingdom for all its status as the one undefeated Western European power, was the one which Churchill actively sought.

When civil servants were discussing Churchill's funeral plans with him, the former Prime Minister insisted that his coffin be brought from London to the family vault in Oxfordshire via Waterloo Station which was a major deviation from the direct route which was via Paddington Station.

When asked why this was so Churchill replied, "Well, if de Gaulle goes before me, I don't suppose it matters. But if de Gaulle is present, it would be good if my coffin could leave London via Waterloo."

De Gaulle said of his relationship with Churchill, "When I am right, I get angry. When he is wrong, he gets angry. We are angry a lot of the time."